Goal in Europe

Michael Hardcastle is a journalist and has written over seventy books for children, most of them about sport, and many specifically on football. He says his own playing career at school was 'completely undistinguished', but he has loyally supported the same football team since he was eleven. He lives near Liverpool.

Also in Armada, featuring Mark Fox:

The First Goal
Breakaway
On the Ball
Shooting Star

Goal in Europe

A Mark Fox Story

Michael Hardcastle

AN ARMADA ORIGINAL

Goal in Europe was first published
as an Armada paperback in 1978
by Fontana Paperbacks,
14 St. James's Place, London SW1A 1PF

© Michael Hardcastle 1978

Printed in Great Britain
by Love & Malcomson Ltd.,
Brighton Road, Redhill, Surrey

CONTENTS

1.	The Letter	*page* 7
2.	Battle at Page Lane	19
3.	The Cup-winners	34
4.	England Expects . . .	43
5.	A Shock for Mark	54
6.	The Dutch Masters	70
7.	Disaster at Thun	87
8.	Operation Red Cross	96
9.	Goal in Europe	108
10.	The Mystery Man	123

Chapter One

THE LETTER

He couldn't believe it. This time, holding the letter close
to his face, he scrutinised the embossed heading, the list of
officials, the quality of the typing, the signature. If it was
a hoax there would surely be some flaw that would give
the game away. He even examined the paper for a water-
mark – but still he wasn't sure what it proved when he
found one.

Mark was thankful that he was alone in his own bedroom so that no one could see that he was trembling with
excitement. For he was beginning to accept that the letter
was perfectly genuine after all. The Football Association
really was inviting him, Mark Fox, to be one of the party
of young players who would travel to Switzerland to
represent England Juniors in a special summer international tournament. The England party was to consist of
sixteen players and the Manager would be Mr Terry
Mercer. Further details would be sent in due course, but,
in the meantime, each player's parents or guardian was
required to give their consent in writing to his son taking
part in the tournament which would be played over a
period of seven to ten days.

It was that one name, Terry Mercer, that had aroused
Mark's suspicions when he first read the letter. For, unless
there were two people in football management called Terry
Mercer, he was the man who was secretary of Rowbay
Sporting Club, a huge sports complex in the West Country

owned by a multi-millionaire. Mark had met him the previous year when, with his friend Albie Jones, he had gone off on what he now preferred to think of as an 'unscheduled' football holiday. In truth, he and Albie had run away following some upheavals at home and misfortune on the football field while playing for Trisham Rovers in the local Saturday Youth League.

They had landed up in Rowbay and had managed to get a game with Sporting Club, who played in the Wessex Vale County League. Mark had played well but it was obvious that Mercer, who also captained the side, hadn't exactly hit it off with Albie.

So, when the letter stated that England Juniors were to be managed by Terry Mercer, Mark's first thought was that the whole thing was a practical joke devised by Albie Jones. Trisham's founder and skipper, a great organiser with an unpredictable sense of humour, was perfectly capable of getting hold of headed notepaper and concocting an official-sounding letter and even arranging for it to be posted in London. He'd get a vast amount of delight out of fooling his best friend.

But Mark was convinced that the letter was authentic. Still clutching it, he fell backwards on to his bed and tried to think about what such a trip would mean to his future as a professional footballer. A great deal would depend on who else was in the tour party, and, particularly who the other strikers were. Earlier in the year he'd played for the South team against the North at Villa Park, Birmingham, so he could make a guess about which of the boys who'd taken part in that match would be going to Switzerland. On the other hand, there were hundreds, possibly thousands, of other promising youngsters from all over the country who must have been considered by the selectors: players Mark had never even heard of, let alone met or seen in action. So, until he'd actually trained with his new team-

mates in the England squad, he couldn't begin to estimate his own chances of being picked for any of the matches in the tournament. He was simply wasting his time thinking about that. The only thing that mattered at the moment was that he had been chosen to go on the tour. That was stupendous – fantastic – magical!

Suddenly, he felt the need for some action, and the desire to tell someone about the news. His parents were the natural choice; they would have to know about it to give their consent. Mark didn't anticipate any difficulties there: his mother, inevitably, would mention her worries about health risks in a foreign country, but, like his father, she would be pleased that he had been chosen to go on tour. But it was *football* details he wanted to discuss at the moment, and, in spite of the support they usually gave to his interests these days, his parents weren't the ones he wanted to talk to on that level. In any case, his father, a telecommunications engineer employed by the Post Office, was working away from home and, as it was Saturday morning, his mother would by now be out shopping.

As he read through the precious letter for the umpteenth time before folding it and slipping it back into the envelope (later it would have a page to itself in his scrapbook), it occurred to him that there was only one person who would be the ideal companion in his present mood: Albie Jones.

Mark rolled off the bed, stowed the letter in the drawer containing his treasured soccer souvenirs, put on a light blue shirt, swept some money into his pocket and hastened downstairs. As he'd suspected, he was the only one left in the house – apart from Mig, his tawny greyhound, who rose eagerly from his basket the moment Mark entered the kitchen.

'Come on, boy, out, out, out!' he called exultantly, reaching for the dog's leash, which was hanging behind the door. 'We've got something to celebrate, Mig! Great news, great news! We're off to Switzerland to play for England!' Effusively, he caressed the beautifully soft muzzle and tweaked Mig's ears.

As he knew it would, the greyhound's exuberance matched his own the instant they were out of the house. When they entered the park he realised that he'd forgotten the tennis ball that normally he carried with him everywhere he went. Mark believed in practising his ball control at every opportunity; the more skilful he was with a small ball, the easier it would be to trap, dribble and hit a football. It often surprised him how many other young players utterly rejected that theory.

Boy and dog bounded across the grass, dog inevitably leading by almost the length of a pitch, and not for the first time Mark wished that Mig had learned to dribble a ball or, better still, make a tackle – professional full-back-style – when Mark was running with the ball. Mig had proved himself to be fairly adaptable at a variety of games, but soccer skills he had never mastered. Not that it mattered this morning: the battered tennis ball had been left behind anyway.

The route across the park was not the shortest way to Albie's home in Derby Road but it enabled Mark to run off some of the excess energy that had been building up inside him since the moment the letter had arrived. Sheer pace, on as well as off the ball, was one of his greatest assets as a striker, and, daily, he went through a regular routine of sprinting exercises. For that exercise alone, Mig was the ideal confederate.

He whistled the dog to heel as they reached the other side of the park. As usual, Mig submitted unwillingly to being leashed. A bus arrived at the stop at precisely the same moment as they did, and the fact that it was Mark's lucky day was confirmed when the driver, recognising him as a frequent passenger, winked broadly and made no charge for the dog.

'See,' whispered Mark, hugging the greyhound into his chest on the bus, 'you're quite popular, too. So don't do anything to disgrace us today. Be nice to Albie. Remember he's had a lot of rotten luck this year.'

Mark was thinking of Albie's double misfortune in breaking his ankle and so being forced to miss the remainder of Rovers' matches during the last weeks of the season. The accident had happened while Albie was attempting to learn to drive; he had turned the car over on an abandoned airfield and his absence from the team was all too evident in Trisham's failure to win the Championship. Still, Mark reflected, Albie was the sort of boy who quickly recovered from disappointments: no doubt he was already keenly planning next season's campaign and working out ways to revitalise and motivate his team. Mark himself was looking forward to resuming his partnership with Albie in the Trisham side. It would have been marvellous if Albie, too, had been picked to go to Switzerland. But there was no likelihood of that: not only was Albie older than Mark, he had never been chosen for any representative side, even at County Schools level.

At the stop nearest to Derby Road, they dropped off the bus and Mig needed no urging to break into a run. There was no answer to the first ring of the bell when they reached Albie's house. Mark experienced a sharp sense of dismay as well as of surprise. But then it occurred to him that he really shouldn't be surprised if Albie wasn't at home at ten o'clock on a Saturday morning at the end of May: his friend wasn't the type to have a lie-in even on a winter Sunday. Most probably he'd gone fishing, his favourite pursuit when he wasn't playing soccer. But where? Mark drilled the bell-push again and prayed that Albie's mother wasn't out.

11

Just as he was on the point of turning away, he heard someone fumbling with the catch and the door opened. His heart sank a little when he saw that it was Mrs Jones.

He had never got on well with her, though he supposed he wasn't alone in that: she seemed to dislike anyone who spent time with her son. Come to that, she rarely showed any affection to Albie himself.

'Oh, it's you again,' she greeted Mark, as though he was forever on her doorstep. 'What do you want this time?'

'Er, is Albie in, Mrs Jones?' he asked as politely as possible, while thinking that she knew very well what he wanted.

'No, he's never in, that boy.' And she started to close the door.

'Then can you please tell me *where* he is,' Mark put in hastily, adding with what he hoped was convincing urgency: 'It really is very important that I have a word with him. Has he gone fishing?'

'Golf club,' she replied tersely. 'That's where he's wasting his time today.'

Before Mark could formulate the next question, the door had shut in his face. He was astonished. The *golf* club? What on earth was Albie doing there? Surely his friend hadn't switched his sporting interests to golf?

Still shaken by disbelief, Mark retreated down the path with Mig, who, of course, didn't mind where they were heading as long as he was on the move with his master.

Luckily, the golf course (Mark assumed it was bound to be the local one) wasn't very far away. When they reached the long drive that led to the half-timbered club house, he wondered what he would answer if anyone in authority asked him where he thought he was going.

To his great surprise, the first person he caught a glimpse of was Albie himself. His friend, briskly crossing the court-yard at the top of the drive, was propelling a golf cart, suitably laden with a bag of clubs, in the direction of the first tee. So, quite obviously, Albie *had* taken up golf! Anxious to catch up with him before he started his round, Mark broke into a run. In such a hallowed spot he was going to risk getting into trouble by yelling at the top of his voice.

However, when he reached the narrow shale pathway that led to the first tee, it was to find that Albie was deep in conversation with an elderly man wearing a grey-and-maroon sweater and window-pane-checked slacks. He had now taken possession of the trolley and was carefully examining a number of golf balls that Albie was holding out to him on the palm of his hand. As Mark watched, the player selected a couple, nodded his approval, slipped them into a pocket of his bag and then gave Albie some coins.

'Thank you, sir, and have a good round,' Albie could be heard saying, as, with a stiff little wave of his hand, the old man moved off to the tee.

The expression on Albie's face was one of benign satisfaction – it was almost a smirk – as he retraced his steps. It hardly changed when he discovered that it was Mark, rather than another golfer-customer, who was waiting for him in the courtyard at the rear of the imposing club house.

'Well, hello, skipper,' he said cheerfully, extending a hand to pat Mig on the head.

'What on earth are you doing here, Albie?' Mark demanded.

'Making some easy money, that's what,' Albie said with a wide grin. 'Easiest money I've ever made, I reckon. I'm deputy acting stand-in caddie-master for the next couple of weeks or so. I fix up caddies for the players and also do a nice line in flogging golf balls. If you fancy a bit of caddie-ing yourself, no problem – though you won't be able to drag Mig round with you. Dogs aren't allowed on the golf

13

course. And while you're out there you can be on the look-out for lost balls. Any you find I'll sell for you and give – '

'Hang on, Albie! I didn't come here to work, I just want a word with you. But I'd still like to know how you managed to get this job.'

'Oh, no problem at all, skipper. Jack Mottram – he's been the caddie-master here for donkey's years – is an old mate of mine. I used to come here searching for lost golf balls when I was a kid and Jack used to pay me for 'em. Well, Jack's had to go into hospital for an operation on his leg – varicose veins – and I offered to stand in for him. He was keen on the idea because it means his job'll still be here for him when he gets back. I organised a squad of young lads to do the caddie-ing and clean the clubs after the players have finished – and, like I said, I sell the balls they find in the rough and the bushes. I just talked my way in to the job, really.'

'You would!' Mark murmured.

'And the captain and the committee reckon I'm doing it better than old Jack himself.' Albie went on, undeterred. 'Could have a permanent number here, if I wanted it. Actually, I'm seriously considering the offer.'

'Until next football season begins, you mean,' Mark pointed out.

Albie shook his head decisively. 'No, no. I'm off football these days. Probably finished with it for good.'

Mark was aghast. 'You're joking,' he said falteringly.

'I'm not, I'm deadly serious,' Albie insisted, folding his arms across his chest as if to buttress his pronouncement.

To Mark, it was like being told that Wembley Stadium had been redeveloped overnight as a housing estate. Without Albie, soccer would never be the same again.

'But why, Albie? Have you got a fatal illness or something? I mean, well, you just can't mean it. You can't give

14

up Trisham Rovers and all the fun you get out of that – and all the great times we've had together.'

This time Albie produced a fairly histrionic sniff. 'Oh, you can give up anything if you've got enough will-power. And I always do what I say I'm going to do. You know that, Mark.' He paused fleetingly, then went on: 'Look, there's no money in soccer unless you get right to the top; and it's also a pretty short life – you're over the top before you're thirty. But golf, well, there's fantastic money in golf. You can make a million dollars just by winning the Open Championship – even quite small tournaments are worth thousands of pounds. So I'm taking up golf, learning all I can from the professional at the club while I'm working here. He reckons I've got a natural aptitude for the game – mind, that doesn't surprise me! And I've plenty of time to get to the top, right to the top. Not in soccer, though.'

He seemed to have run out of words at last. But then, before Mark could make any response, he added an afterthought: 'I haven't had the lucky breaks you've had, Mark. Getting picked for representative matches and so on, and then getting that offer from Athletic. I expect that's what you came to see me about, isn't it? Made up your mind yet to sign for them?'

To his own considerable astonishment, Mark suddenly realised that not even once that morning had he thought about the invitation he'd received from Athletic, the local First Division club. It had come several weeks earlier, following a match in London when he'd played brilliantly for County Schools. For months he'd been hoping that a leading club would want him to sign associated schoolboy forms for them, and his fingers were crossed that it would be either Chelsea or Everton, his favourite teams. But no one had approached him until the Athletic coach had turned up quite out of the blue.

Normally, Mark would have been thrilled to gain the attention of any First Division club: the one exception, though, was Athletic. Mark's elder brother, Barry, had been on their books until he was injured in his first game for the Reserves, and Athletic had, in his mother's words, 'sold him off like a bundle of old clothes'. Mrs Fox remained very bitter about the whole business, maintaining that Barry had been treated very shabbily. Barry had eventually moved to a non-League side after weeks of indecision. Now, though, he seemed reasonably happy with life once more.

'Well, the family are a bit divided about what I should do,' Mark explained to Albie. 'You know, after the troubles Barry had with Athletic, Mum is dead set against the idea, but Dad, well, he understands how *I* feel about things. After all, we're talking about *my* future. I might never get another invitation from a top club. So I don't intend to miss out on this one if I can help it.'

'Yeah, see what you mean,' Albie said with sympathy. 'Still, you don't have to decide right away, do you? Especially as the season's just about finished. Like you say, nobody else is exactly chasing you for a signature.'

Mark hesitated, then took the plunge. 'Well, er, they might be – if I really hit top form in Switzerland. Bound to be plenty of club managers watching us out there.'

He waited to see what effect those words would have on his friend – and he wasn't disappointed.

'Switzerland! You're going to Switzerland? Who with?' Albie was astounded.

'Invitation arrived this morning. From the Football Association. I've been picked for the England Juniors' squad to take part in an international tournament next month. Fantastic, isn't it?'

Albie drew breath sharply, then expelled it slowly. 'Honestly, some guys have all the flaming luck! Still, I reckon you deserve it, Mark, I'll say that. You've been playing some good stuff this season – for every team except Trisham Rovers, that is!'

Mark laughed. That was more like the old Albie. It had really bothered him to find his best friend in such an anti-football mood. But that, he felt sure, was merely a temporary attitude. Come the start of the new season and Antony Albert Jones, captain and coach and organiser-in-chief of Trisham Rovers, would be rarin' to go again, determined as ever to lead Rovers right to the top. Boys as soccer-mad as Albie didn't switch their deepest allegiances overnight.

'Hey,' Mark continued in happier vein, 'guess who's been made Manager of the team – the touring party I mean. Your old mate from Rowbay, Terry Mercer!'

Albie didn't even raise an eyebrow. 'That doesn't surprise me. Just the sort of job he would land. He's as ambitious as you are, more so, if anything. But you'll have to watch him, Mark.'

'Oh? What does that mean?'

'Well, it was pretty obvious to me at Rowbay that he'll do anything, sacrifice anybody, to get right to the top. I'll bet he's already worked out that this job as tour manager is just the first step up the ladder to the England Manager's job. So once he's started climbing he won't let anything stand in his way. That's how I read Mister Terry Mercer.'

'Are you sure you aren't, well, just a bit prejudiced because you didn't hit it off with him at Rowbay, Albie? I know you think he just made use of us when we believed he was doing us a good turn.'

Albie was perfectly willing to consider that point of view. But then he shook his head firmly.

'Don't think so, Mark. You know me. I can usually sum a guy up, see what makes him tick. That's why I'm warning you to play it cool with him. If things go wrong he'll be looking for scapegoats. He'll be determined to see that his own precious reputation doesn't suffer, no matter what happens to anyone else.'

Mark shrugged. 'Maybe. But then, we'll all be playing for ourselves, won't we? We'll be playing as a team to win, but we'll also be playing as individuals. That's inevitable because every player on the tour will be thinking about how it will affect his future career. I know I will.'

'Do you know many of the other players? Anybody in the squad that I might know?'

'I don't know who else has been picked, Albie. Wish I did because then I'd know what my chances were of playing in the first game. But there wasn't a list of names or anything like that in the letter I got.'

Pointedly, Albie looked at his watch – and raised both eyebrows. 'Look, Mark, I'd like to go on nattering with you but I've work to do. The next players are due to arrive any minute and I've got to get their clubs ready. Can't keep 'em waiting, you know!'

Nodding his understanding, Mark tugged gently at the leash to bring Mig to his feet. 'Yeah, the hound here needs some more exercise so I'd better be going myself. See you, Albie.'

He was already several metres down the drive when there was a yell from Albie. 'Best of luck on the tour, skipper! Oh, and I hope you stick a few in the net for Hedger's in the Cup Final. Next week, isn't it?'

'Yes, that's right. Thanks, Albie.'

For the second time that morning Mark was startled to find that he had completely forgotten something else that was vitally important in his football life – and he almost tripped over the leash as he turned again towards the exit.

The match which Mark had contrived to relegate to the back of his mind, and which Albie had remembered, was the County Schools' Knock-Out Cup Final between

Hedger's and Zeeland Comprehensive at Page Lane Sports Arena. It was being played so late in the season because of difficulties in arranging some of the earlier fixtures; but, if anything, the delay had intensified the fierce rivalry that had long existed between the two schools who had reached the Final. Hedger's had never before reached that stage of the competition, whereas Zeeland had twice won the trophy.

For Mark it would be the first Cup Final of any description in which he had taken part and he coveted a winner's medal. Scoring the winning goal for Hedger's would be, he reflected, the perfect way of rounding off the season in England before he made his international debut on foreign soil.

Chapter Two

BATTLE AT PAGE LANE

It was a scorchingly hot day, a foretaste of a glorious summer. Spectators, arriving by the bus-load up to an hour before kick-off, were discarding shirts and thinking about getting a suntan. Talk about the teams they'd come to support took second place to the weather. It was, as someone remarked, the sort of day you'd expect for a Test match between England and Australia – in Australia.

Hedger's had won the toss for choice of dressing-rooms and, naturally, picked the home team's in the expectation that it would be the more comfortable and better equipped of the two; and they were right. There Derek Vernmore, the tall and powerfully-built captain, was pacing up and down, wearing only abbreviated briefs.

He'd always enjoyed displaying his physique, particularly in front of the junior members of the team, but at the moment his mind was more on the game than on his muscles. Like everyone else, he was waiting for Ted Bayley, the school's sports master, to put in an appearance. Bayley's tactical talks never contained much original thought, but in recent weeks the boys had been infected by his confidence in their ability to overwhelm the opposition. His absence now, with less than ten minutes to go to kick-off, had put some of them on edge. Following the same routine was an important part of the build-up to a match.

Mark was feeling quite calm: no trace of the pre-match nerves that usually affected him just before taking the field for a crucial game. He wasn't really sure why he should feel so relaxed, especially as he knew that the team were going to depend heavily on his skills. They always did, even though Derek liked to make out that no member of the side was better than another – with the exception of himself, of course.

All the same, the news of Mark's selection for the England Juniors' tour party had deliberately been 'leaked' with the aim of sowing dismay and apprehension in the ranks of the Zeeland players. Mark was well aware that such a move was bound to result in him being watched at closely as a Mafia victim in the rush hour: but he was used to that sort of treatment from opponents, and tight marking hadn't prevented him from scoring ten goals in previous rounds of the Cup. He supposed that his un-worried state was due to his knowledge that he had nothing to prove in the game: *he* was the only player who was going to Switzerland. His reputation had been enhanced even before a ball was kicked. Zeeland were the ones who had most to worry about because they were the favourites and had set their hearts on completing a hat-trick of Cup Final victories.

Brian Torson, who had replaced Mark as the youngest member of the team and played alongside him as a very speedy left-winger, came to sit beside his partner on the bench.

'How're you feeling, Mark?' he asked.

'Fine. You?'

Mark didn't really have to ask: it was very obvious indeed that Brian was extremely nervous. Brian, who was half Danish, was clasping and unclasping his hands behind his neck and continuously running his tongue along his teeth.

'A bit worked up,' he admitted candidly.

'As soon as you've worked up some pace on the wing and turned their full-back inside-out, you'll feel great,' Mark grinned. 'Jackie or I'll make sure you get an early feel of the ball. Once the game's started, all you'll think about is the winner's medal you're going to get! That's for sure.'

Brian managed a weak smile. Jackie Newland, who'd been watching him, produced a huge wink and a thumb's up gesture. An aggressive wing-half and renowned ball-winner, Jackie provided the springboard for many of the team's attacks. Like Mark, he hoped to play for England one day, but so far he hadn't caught the interest of selectors at any level. Mark thought that Jackie had just been unlucky. He had the disadvantage that he wasn't a spectacular player: he got through his work with formidable, but quiet, efficiency.

Then there was a stir in the corridor and, at last, in bustled Ted Bayley. He looked grave. Suddenly, and unaccountably, Mark experienced the onset of nervousness. Had the sports master learned something about Zeeland that would swing the match their way? Undeniably, Mr Bayley appeared troubled. But his manner was brisk enough.

'Right, lads, this is it,' he began rather fatuously, standing in the centre of the room. 'What we've all been working for. The culmination of all our hard work.'

'The *team's* hard work, you mean,' Jackie murmured. The remark must have been audible to Bayley but he chose to ignore it.

'I have no doubt at all that we're going to win, just so long as we all play together *as a team*. Play for each other, not for personal glory.'

Mark sensed that this comment was directed at him. Ted Bayley's attitude to Mark alternated between open admiration of his skills and apparent resentment of his successes in winning representative honours. Jackie Newland had a theory that Bayley was jealous of Mark because the sports master himself had never achieved any kind of fame. There was also a belief that Ted's varying moods were a direct result of his domestic problems. For the moment, though, there could be no doubt that his one ambition was to see Hedger's carry off the Schools' Cup.

'I *know* you've got the beating of this opposition,' he was continuing. 'They have a couple of useful lads in the forward line – Parker and Wakeman – but their defence doesn't amount to much. Their right-back is especially ponderous, so he should be easy meat for you, Brian.'

Young Torson managed another tentative smile. Mark suspected that Ted Bayley had dreamed up that description in order to give Brian confidence. Well, that was all right unless the Zeeland full-back proved to be a budding international in top form. In that event, Brian's confidence would melt like ice under a sunray lamp.

'There is one other thing I must say, boys. I've just been talking to the headmaster. As you'd expect, he's terrifically keen to see Hedger's win the Cup. But, above all else, he wants our reputation for fair play to be enhanced. Good sportsmanship must come before everything else. Those were his words.'

'Oh, the heck with that!' exploded Derek Vernmore. 'We've come here for the medals, not the Order of Chivalry!'

Even Derek must have been gratified by the instant and genuine burst of laughter which greeted that response.

Ted Bayley didn't share the amusement. 'Derek, the headmaster's wishes must be respected. Moreover, it's going to be very hot out there, so it's even more important that no one loses his temper or does something stupid. Don't be provoked into retaliation. Keep cool, play it cool.'

'And play up, play up the school!' quipped Jackie Newland.

'That's right,' agreed Mr Bayley, much to Jackie's surprise. He'd expected a sardonic reprimand for such an attempt at levity. The sports master looked at his watch.

'Right, lads, thirty seconds to get out there. I shall be leading you on to the pitch and then there'll be the official presentation to the chairman of the Schools' F.A. So this is my last chance to wish you the best of luck. Remember, I expect us all to be celebrating tonight.'

Mark decided that probably it had been sensible of Ted to leave things to the last minute. Now they all had to hurry to finish changing. It would look bad if the team were late on to the pitch. Mark pulled on his shorts and shirt – Hedger's played in an all-light-blue strip, a colour that greatly appealed to him – and then ran a comb through his thick, dark-brown hair. Derek, he noticed, was actually slapping on some after-shave lotion.

Jackie had also spotted that. 'At least he won't taste so bad if we have to kiss him for scoring a goal!' he cracked.

23

The referee, a small man with a mass of iron-grey hair, poked his head into the dressing-room and said loudly: 'Time to go, lads.'

Ted Bayley was waiting for them as they emerged from the room and led them on to the pitch in Indian-file, Wembley-fashion. The cheering from the fans had already started and it reached a crescendo as the two teams came into view. Zeeland, in white shorts and red shirts, seemed to have the edge in popular support: but then they were a bigger school than Hedger's.

Mark, for one, would have liked to start kicking a ball about immediately, but first the Finalists had to line up with the officials on the halfway line for a handshake from the chairman of the S.F.A. All that the ceremony seemed to lack was the sound of the National Anthem. Mark smiled to himself: he was thinking that he'd probably enjoy that experience in Switzerland.

'Have a good game,' the chairman said to Mark, giving him a single, brisk shake of the hand. Mark smiled his thanks. He knew he wasn't receiving preferential treatment: the Chairman was saying exactly the same words to every player.

Mark glanced round at the crowd. It would be the biggest any of them had played in front of and the ground was still filling up as latecomers arrived. Somewhere among all those people would be his grandfather, Ralph Blackshaw, who had promised that nothing would keep him from attending Mark's first Cup Final. Mark hoped that Grandad, a former professional player who had spent most of his career with a Third Division club, wasn't going to suffer from the effects of the heat.

The preliminaries over, the teams broke away to opposite ends of the pitch. Instead of shooting-in, however, the Zeeland players began to pose for group and individual photographs. The cameraman was a sixth-former and seemed to have an extensive range of equipment and props, including a rather gaudy motor-cyclist's crash helmet which some of the players put on for jokey pictures. Their goalkeeper, Corwin, was rumoured to be on Walsall's books already, and was built, in Jackie Newland's not very original phrase, like a barn door. Sporting that crash helmet he looked an even more formidable proposition for opposing forwards. All in all, Zeeland gave the impression of being as confident as they were relaxed. So much, Mark reflected, for the theory that they're going to worry about me!

Derek Vernmore, after winning the toss, took a calculating look at the angle of the sun to the pitch and then chose to play towards the Page Lane end. To Mark, that wasn't a shrewd decision: he would have preferred to kick off and keep possession as long as possible, especially as the effect of the sun would remain the same throughout the match unless the weather changed melodramatically.

As it was, Wakeman, a stocky and bouncy striker, instantly sowed dismay among Hedger's defenders. Bustling through the middle on the ball from Parker's pass, he fended off an impulsive tackle by the centre-half and then, very skilfully, dummied past Jackie Newland. Zeeland's supporters were in full cry already and the crescendo of sound must have been pure magic to Wakeman. With a splendid change of pace he hurtled towards the penalty area. Hedger's goalkeeper, Bobby Storr, was now jumping up and down on his line in dire alarm, screaming for cover. The situation was hardly of panic proportions, but Bobby's nerves seemed to be in poor shape.

Wakeman was eager to exploit his advantage . . . too eager. As he reached the edge of the box he slowed, swivelled and hit a left-foot shot towards the top far corner of the net. The ball was undoubtedly going to fly just wide of the upright but Storr wasn't taking any chances. Instead of watching it pass over the line he leaped to punch it away. He made contact with the ball but merely succeeded in altering its direction: it richocheted from his knuckles and skimmed the crossbar. Bobby sagged in relief at giving away a corner. Punching had always been his weakness; he could be both brave and agile but no one had managed to convince him that the ball should be grabbed rather than fisted away in the great majority of cases. On more than one occasion his punch had deflected a shot into the net, but even that hadn't cured him. Unfortunately, Hedger's hadn't another goalkeeper of the right age who could match the skills that Bobby did possess.

Predictably, Derek Vernmore stormed into the penalty area for a fierce word with Storr and a general demand to his side to 'settle down, settle down!' He would add his own height to the defensive set-up, but, for once, it wasn't the opposing centreforward that he had to mark. For Parker had gone over to take the kick himself. It turned out to be a beauty.

The ball came in hard and quite low to the near post, taking Hedger's right-back by complete surprise. Wakeman, however, had anticipated such a move: darting out to it, he ducked and back-headed it into the box. Zeeland's commanding centre-half rose above everyone – out-jumping even Vernmore – and flicked it sideways. Inevitably, Bobby Storr had rushed out, fist raised, but before he could connect with the ball an attacker thrust himself forward and chested it into the net.

Page Lane Sports Arena erupted – or, rather, approximately sixty per cent of the crowd erupted. A goal within a minute of the kick-off was even better than Zeeland supporters had hoped for in their wildest imaginings. 'Zee-land, Zee-land,' reverberated round the stadium for what seemed like minutes on end. All that was missing

26

from the display of ecstasy was an invasion of the pitch: but week-long threats from the heads of both schools of the severest punishment for offenders were being heeded.

Naturally, Vernmore led the protests to the referee: surely, surely, the official must have seen that the scorer *handled* the ball? Nonsense, retorted the referee, the goal was perfectly legitimate. 'Let's get on with the game, Hedger's – unless . . .' That threat didn't need to be voiced. After all, the referee's hand had already strayed towards the pocket where he kept his notebook and the coloured cards to display to offenders.

Derek sensibly turned away, but he gesticulated furiously all the way back to the centre circle. Mark trotted across to line up beside him. He was as shaken as everyone else by the disaster that had stuck his team. There couldn't be a worse way in which to start a Cup Final. The one place he daren't glance at was the touchline where Ted Bayley was importantly occupying the trainer's bench. Ted would be seething. Unless Hedger's swiftly cancelled out that goal and then took the lead they'd all suffer at half-time.

It was Derek who insisted on receiving the ball at kick-off, and Mark wasn't at all surprised to see him try to copy Wakeman. On his day, Hedger's skipper could show some deft footwork, but his real strengths lay in his determination and shooting. He almost lost the ball the moment he was tackled and that appeared to make him think again about going it alone: so he whacked the ball out to the right wing and his favourite colleague, Jerry Rendell. The winger had been improving all season and was now perfectly willing to take on an opponent as well as demonstrate his speed.

Mark spurted forward on a parallel track, hoping eventually for a cross-field pass. Even in such high noon

27

conditions his shadow was soon apparent. As Mark ran, a Zeeland midfield player kept pace with him within touching distance. Mark skidded to a halt; so did his marker. Brian Torson, however, had gone flying by on the outside of them like an inter-city express. Rendell, beating one man, pivoted and sent the ball looping into the middle. Vernmore, obviously mesmerised by the way in which Zeeland had scored their goal, imitated their tactic by back-heading the ball across the line of the penalty area. Doubtless he had assumed that Mark would be close at hand to snap it up. But Mark had only just started to move again.

Torson was still travelling at high speed when the ball came towards him at an acute angle. He slowed, turned, and then, because the full-back was also going for the ball, lunged at it. He missed it completely and cannoned into his opponent who promptly fell flat on his back. The referee charged up, waving an admonitory finger at Brian and awarded a free kick against Hedger's. The full-back, now on his feet again, ceased to look aggrieved and took the kick himself.

'Just tell your lads to calm down,' the referee murmured to Vernmore as he passed him. 'I won't stand for any rough stuff. A Final is supposed to be an exhibition game.'

'Some exhibition *you're* giving,' Derek muttered, almost audibly. Then he turned his wrath on Mark. 'Get up front, Fox, where I can find you. You're supposed to be a striker not a sweeper. You can't expect me to win this game on my own against this lot.'

Mark shrugged. Derek, he could tell, was back to his usual form: ready to bite the hand that could feed him the goals he so desperately wanted to score himself. Before long, no doubt, he would be reminding Mark that a budding international was supposed to bloom some day, so why not let his alleged talent flower sooner rather than later. Derek could be quite good with the metaphors when he was on form.

Zeeland seemed intent on slowing the game down. A goal to the good, they could afford to take their time in building for the next assault. The pressure was on Hedger's: so let them run themselves into the ground in the heat. In the coolest fashion, Zeeland were knocking the ball around, making Hedger's chase. Only Wakeman was regularly galvanised into swift action. He delighted in taking on defenders, two or more at a time, and Newland was having a wretched time trying to restrain him.

To Mark, Zeeland's tactics were all wrong. They had the initiative and they should be seeking to add to their lead. Another goal for them before half-time and they would have at least one hand on the Cup. He dropped back to assist Jackie to neutralise Wakeman's solo endeavours. He was well aware that Vernmore would rage about his disobedience but that couldn't be helped. In any case, Mark was taking his shadow with him and thus helping to pull Zeeland's tightly-knit defence apart.

Suddenly, he had the slice of luck he needed. Jackie went into another crunching tackle on Wakeman and this time made contact with the ball. But, as he tried to drag it away into an open space, Wakeman stuck out a leg and managed to flick the ball away from his opponent. It rolled straight into Mark's path.

Two of Mark's greatest assets were his ball control and his electric initial pace when he made a run. Now he used both. Anticipating that the ball might come his way, he'd already pulled clear of his glue-like opponent. With a surge of acceleration he drew right away, heading straight for goal. A real Fox run was always an exhilarating sight for his team's supporters and for once it was the chant 'Hed-ger's', Hed-ger's' which gained ascendancy in the sound waves.

29

As a defender thrust towards him, intent on checking the attack at almost any cost, Mark feinted to go one way, turned the other, and then, pushing the ball past the man on that side, raced past him on his original track to pick the ball up again. The chanting, mixed now with roars of approval, intensified. Most of his school-mates and his team-mates expected him to cut right into the penalty area and shoot from close range, especially now that Zeeland's defence was in such disarray.

Mark hadn't so much as glanced towards the wing where, he knew, Brian Torson was in position to accept a pass. Mark was more concerned with the progress of Derek Vernmore who was powering up the middle of the park. On the occasions when he really stirred himself Derek could produce a lot of speed. This was one of those occasions. With faultless timing and judgment, Mark swung his left foot and swept the ball to the point that Derek would reach in the next couple of strides.

Almost everyone who'd seen Derek regularly in action expected him to take the ball to the edge of the box and hammer in a shot. He didn't. Retaining the ball for only a stride and a half, he then flicked it out to the right flank – and kept running. Jerry Rendell, also the recipient of a perfect pass, immediately cut past the full-back on the inside and then slid the ball diagonally into the penalty area.

The entire movement, from the moment Mark gathered the ball in his own half of the field, had been flowing and beautiful. It was going to be rounded off just as handsomely it seemed. Hedger's skipper zeroed on to the ball again, steadied himself for the shot that was going to bring his team the equaliser, and then hit it with rare precision as Corwin, the goalkeeper, dithered just off his line. Vernmore had aimed for a spot just inside the base of the far post and the ball scarcely rose above the turf. Belatedly, Corwin dived but had no hope of reaching it.

It was going to be a goal all the way.

Derek had already flung his arms upwards to signal his triumph when the ball struck some object and rebounded into play. Zeeland's right-back, who had been guarding Brian Torson until it was obvious the winger wasn't going to be involved in the movement, was dashing into the box as the ball bounced towards him. Instinctively, he tried to hook it away and succeeded only in lofting it over the dead-ball line.

Momentarily, Derek froze, totally unable to believe his eyes. Then, feverishly, he sought the referee. He wasn't the only one to demand justice from the official: in moments all the Hedger's players, apart from Bobby Storr, were clustered round him, clamouring for the goal to be awarded.

The referee, scissoring fiercely with his arms, tried to break out of the ring. It was impossible. Derek was so incensed he even grabbed the man's arm as if trying to calm *him* down.

'It must be a goal, must be!' Derek was yelling. 'The ball was in the net – it must have been in the net to hit that, that damned crash helmet. They'd no right to leave that helmet there! So it must be a goal.'

'No goal! The whole of the ball didn't cross the line,' the official pronounced decisively. 'Stop arguing. It'll – '

'But if that helmet – ' Mark started to say.

'Players should read the rules, lad,' the referee retorted. 'A goal cannot be allowed if the ball has been prevented, by some outside agent, from passing over the goal-line. That's the law. That helmet constitutes an outside agent. Play must be re-started by dropping the ball by the goal-line where the interference took place.'

Rather to his own surprise, the referee's statement

31

temporarily silenced the protesters. Then, rather unwisely, he added: 'Sorry, but you've just been unlucky. I'll have a word with that goalkeeper.'

The babble resumed instantly as the 'unlucky' players streamed after the referee. 'That's not bad luck, that's diabolical injustice,' Derek was screaming. 'You can't just rub my goal out because of a stupid obstruction!'

But that was what the referee had done. Corwin appeared suitably chastened after listening to the referee's stern disapproval, and he removed the offending helmet from the net. The photographer-owner darted forward to retrieve it before Jerry Rendell could kick it out of the ground. Then, inevitably, the referee had to issue threats of dire punishment before the Hedger's players calmed down.

Because of his fury, Derek hadn't realised that he still had an excellent chance of getting the ball into the net. It was only when the ref, ball tucked under his arm summoned him to the goal-line that he grasped the situation. For, as the ref now indicated, the ball was going to be dropped right on the line; therefore, the Zeeland players would be unable to place themselves between the ball and their goal. So the odds were stacked in favour of Hedger's.

Normally, the defending players would have made at least a token objection to having the ball dropped so close to the danger zone. The Zeeland team were simply mightily relieved that they still led by a goal. Their captain assembled his men along the line, with Corwin ready to drop on the ball if he had the chance. Derek Vernmore, of course, was the most eager to put the boot in first and so be credited with the goal that for the rest of his life he would believe he had scored the last time he kicked the ball.

The ball dropped . . . boots were already lashing out

. . . someone grunted with pain as he took a kick on the knee . . . Corwin was already falling heavily into the midst of the melée . . . the ball bounced off a thigh . . . it struck Corwin's flailing arm . . . shot up high into the air . . . clipped the crossbar . . . and fell on to the roof of the net for a corner kick.

'Oh no, no, no,' Derek moaned disbelievingly. He sank his face into his hands and seemed about to weep with sheer frustration.

Mark reacted swiftly. Knocking the ball off the netting, he raced down to the corner flag as the referee hurriedly resumed his normal role. He was more anxious than anyone that the game should continue without further controversy. He couldn't admit it to anyone but he knew he was at fault in not having checked the goal-lines – both of them – for possible obstructions. His immediate sympathy was with Hedger's, but he had to apply the rules of the game.

The kick came over as Derek was emerging from his private agony. He saw the ball but was too late to jump for it. With gratitude, Zeeland's captain headed it firmly out of the box and a team-mate in midfield thumped it into the opposite half of the field.

Within a minute, the second goal of the match had been scored.

Of all twenty-two players, the one least affected by the drama of the no-goal incident was the irrepressible Wakeman. When, as Zeeland mounted their next attack, the ball reached him on the right wing, he dallied with it for several seconds, forcing Jackie Newland to attempt to dispossess him. Then, as Jackie rushed in, Wakeman impertinently pushed the ball between the defender's legs, sped after it, exchanged a brisk one-two with the attendant Parker and drove a fierce shot into the net between Storr's body and the near post.

33

B

It was a breath-taking, audacious goal and Zeeland's supporters rose to acclaim it *en masse*. There was no doubt in their minds that Wakeman had now won the Cup for them.

The cheers were still ringing round the arena as the referee signalled the end of the first half.

Mark, in common with most of his team-mates, felt like slumping to the ground and staying there. The last place they wanted to be was in the dressing-room.

Chapter Three

THE CUP-WINNERS

His face was like a thundercloud. Never had any of them seen Ted Bayley so thoroughly angry. It was enough to calm them all down. As they sipped orange drinks or tea, he stood in the middle of the dressing-room, pounding fist into palm.

'To be penalised for *their* deplorable conduct in littering the goalmouth with rubbish, it's beyond belief! But I'll have that referee if it's the last thing I do, I'll have him. He won't referee another game if I can help it. His career's over, finished, kaput!'

Mark, as entranced as everyone else by this display of righteous fury, wondered where Ted had picked up that word. He was surprised that the master was going on so much about the disallowed goal; as their coach he should really be getting them to think about their game, motivating them for the second half. Mark had to suppress a grin as he imagined what the headmaster would have to say if he could hear Ted's outburst. It would hardly accord with the head's views on good sportsmanship. On the other hand, Mr Bayley could afford to concentrate on that one incident because it provided him with the perfect excuse if Hedger's failed to win the Cup: they had been *cheated* out of success.

Someone had the sense to offer the sports master a cool drink. He took it, stopped talking to sip at it, and then let his gaze travel slowly round the room.

It came to rest on Jackie Newland, lying full-length on the bench and gently fanning himself with a newspaper.

'You're feeling a trifle hot, are you, Newland?' he inquired politely.

'A bit. But not as hot as you are – sir.'

'Oh, I see, we're able to make little jokes about our plight, are we?' Bayley said very precisely through clenched teeth. 'Well, that's very comforting for us all, especially coming from you, Newland, the one player who's got us into this mess. I'm quite surprised you're not wearing a red shirt, the way you've been giving the game to the opposition.'

'That's not fair!' Jackie exploded, jerking himself into a sitting position.

'Not fair? No, you're right, Newland. Nothing's fair about this game. It's the most unfair, one-sided contest I've ever seen.' Ted Bayley paused and then raised his voice again. 'It's not fair on me, on the school, or anyone who supports you. You haven't got into the game yet, any of you. You're all standing around admiring the way *they're* playing. Look, in precisely one minute you're going out there again, and I want you to *fight* for this cup, *fight* with every ounce of energy you've got, with every atom of skill you're supposed to possess. You're going to *hurl* yourselves at them the moment the whistle sounds.

Fall on them like a ton of bricks. Flatten 'em. That's what you're going to do.'

'That's what they'll expect us to do, go at them like mad to get a goal back,' Mark said quietly. 'They'll try to contain us, bound to.'

'Oh, then you can think of some better tactics for us to employ, young Fox?' The sports master's sarcasm had definitely re-surfaced. Yet it was surprisingly mild, as Mark himself recognised.

'Er, no – no, we've obviously got to attack.'

'If you don't, I doubt that any of you will ever play for Hedger's again.'

When the game resumed, the ecstatic Zeeland supporters were cheering every time one of their players touched the ball. The red-shirted team seemed every bit as keen as their opponents on attacking, and, far from pulling men back, they were eager to send their midfield players to join the assault force lead by the redoubtable Wakeman. So the uncommitted spectators – if any were present – were treated to some rousing end-to-end play of the kind beloved by sports writers. For practically the first time, Brian Torson made a positive contribution to the match with a well-controlled run along the touchline. Derek Vernmore, showing surprising mobility in this match, was the one who went out to help him. From a tussle close by the corner flag, Derek emerged with the ball. Spotting Mark just outside the box, he hammered the ball towards him.

It reached Mark at hip-height. Killing it on his thigh, he half-turned, and then, employing one of his favourite gambits, back-heeled the ball for Jackie Newland to run on to and, with luck, seize an opening. Jackie possessed a really powerful shot when he hit the ball well – and this time he connected perfectly. But Corwin, who so far had had little to do in the match, showed his worth by fielding the shot easily. He took the ball with both hands above his head, tossed it up again, advanced a couple of steps and then booted the ball upfield with a very confident air. That earned him some extra cheers; although he wasn't aware of the fact, he was already, in the eyes of most supporters, one of his team's heroes as a result of that now notorious 'helmet save'.

Mark grimaced. If only Jackie had shown a little patience and taken the ball on for a few more strides he'd surely have scored – and Hedger's would have been back in the game.

Derek stalked back down the centre of the pitch, his expression perfectly conveying his exasperation at the follies and weaknesses of his team-mates. For once, Mark thoroughly sympathised with him. Derek was playing better, and less selfishly, than usual, but the team as a whole was having a bad game. Mark himself was feeling rather sluggish and he suspected that it had little to do with the heat of the day. It had been a long, hard season for him in a variety of competitions – the Saturday Youth League, the Schools' Cup, representative games for County Schools and other organisations – and so he had reason to feel jaded. Nonetheless, he found the situation rather alarming; after all, when he became a professional foot-baller the seasons would be even more crowded, especially if his club were competing in Europe and had a good run in the F.A. Cup.

Idly, he glanced towards the packed terraces. Some-where among all those people would be two men with a particular interest in his performance in this match: his grandfather, and the scout from Athletic. He didn't know for certain that anyone from Athletic would be keeping an eye on him but it seemed likely now that the club was showing such interest in him. Suddenly, it occurred to Mark that Athletic might well decide that Zeeland's aggressive striker, Wakeman, possessed more potential than Mark Fox. It couldn't be denied, Mark realised, that so far he himself had accomplished nothing in this Cup Final. If he was to make a telling contribution to the game it would have to be soon: time was running out.

Mark hurried away in search of the ball. To find it, he had to drop back deep into his own half, for Zeeland were continuing to mount carefully-constructed attacks. Even though they had every reason to believe that the Cup was going to be theirs, Zeeland had no intention of simply sitting on their lead. On each previous occasion they'd won the Cup it had been by a single goal. They were determined that this time the margin was going to be a good deal wider.

It gave Mark great satisfaction to take the ball off Wakeman with a sliding tackle which earned him some applause from Hedger's supporters. They'd really had nothing to cheer about so far. Wakeman, as determined as a demolition truck driver on overtime rates, was soon back in action and put in a cleverly-flighted centre which Bobby Storr was obliged to finger-tip over the bar. Mark stationed himself on the edge of the penalty area for the corner kick – and was lucky enough to be exactly in the right place to pick it up when the ball was headed away to safety.

Evading a challenging Zeeland midfield player, Mark set off at a good clip towards the halfway line. Because he was a left-flank striker – he was the only naturally left-footed player in the entire team – his fellow forwards, as well as the opposition, supposed he would eventually move in that direction. Mark went in a straight line until, neatly hurdling an opponent's leg as the boy made a lungeing tackle, he suddenly veered away to the right. Zeeland's distracted defence was now uncertain what action to take to cut him off. Jerry Rendell was equally bewildered: was he to keep to his own wing for a one-two with Mark or should he cut inside? Mark, sensing that all this confusion was to his advantage, gave no indication to anyone of what he was about to attempt.

A change of gear, a burst of rare speed, and he was clear on the right touch-line. Jerry Rendell decided it was the moment for him to go into the middle, and the left-back went with him. Derek Vernmore, believing that glory was about to arrive after all, edged leftwards, signalling to Brian Torson to be ready for something but to stay on-side. Mark slowed and then began to jig sideways, rolling the ball along with his left instep or the sole of his boot. An opponent, despatched from defence, came at him and Mark halted, baiting him with the ball.

As another defender advanced behind the first Mark was on the move again, flicking the ball over his nearest opponent's foot while keeping it close as possible to the by-line. Now supporters were beginning to chant his name as he headed, apparently, for the corner flag. Glancing up he saw, much to his surprise, that Zeeland's defence still hadn't re-grouped – and that Vernmore was inclining further to the left with Jerry Rendell and Brian Torson slicing into the middle from opposite directions.

With yet another change of direction, one which completely threw the second-line defender, who'd been convinced that Fox was about to centre the ball, Mark sped for the dead-ball line. Corwin, the goalkeeper, began to sidle towards the near post, ready to reduce the space to be aimed at if the attacker tried a shot. Mark reached the line, midway between corner flag and goal post, showed the ball to a now understandably wary full-back, pulled it back under his toes, turned away from the goalmouth in a half circle and then, with his left foot, lifted the ball over to the far side of the box – and, continuing his momentum, raced after it.

Derek, unhampered by the proximity of any Zeeland player, rose superbly and, with timing that was just as good, headed the ball towards the top of the net. Corwin flung himself back and sideways. The ball was beyond the goalkeeper's reach. But it didn't enter the net. It snapped against the crossbar and then, following a lazy arc, it fell back towards the penalty spot.

Mark, who hadn't stopped running, flung himself head-long at the ball before it could reach the ground. The net was wide open and he should have found it: *would have* but for Corwin's instantaneous reaction. Although seemingly still off balance, with one knee still pressed into the turf as he was picking himself up, the goalkeeper launched himself to his right. With his right arm at full stretch he somehow managed to divert the ball high over the bar and into the crowd.

For Corwin it was the save of the whole season and his team-mates treated it as such. Momentarily, he vanished from sight under the hail of praise.

Mark lay prone, deflated by his efforts and misfortune in not scoring. He had suspected from a point quite early in the match that this was going to be neither Hedger's day nor his. Now he could prove it. Jackie Newland was the one who came up to drag him to his feet before Brian Torson took the corner kick.

'Unbelievable, unbelievable,' Jackie was muttering, shaking his head at every syllable. Mark couldn't speak. In any case, there was nothing to say. Corwin's fantastic save had said everything.

Brian's kick was rather feeble, but Derek was able to make contact with the ball and stab it towards Mark, who was alert enough again to spot an opening. He lobbed the ball adroitly to the gap by the far post – and Corwin, grinning like a successful bank robber, sprang into the space to clutch it comfortably. Mark swung round and trudged away as the ball, from the goalie's drop kick, soared over his head and down-field.

With less than two minutes of the match remaining, Parker, who'd worked selflessly for his side, received the ball just inside Hedger's half. Taking it on only a few paces, he then sent Wakeman away with a delightfully-chipped pass. And Wakeman, whose day it most certainly was, waltzed through an almost transfixed defence to plant the ball in the back of the net.

Undeniably, it was the perfect way to win a Cup Final.

Jackie was standing beside Mark as they lined up for their losers' medals.

'Well, I'd like to hear our Ted explain away this defeat,' he remarked matter-of-factly. 'He said he had no doubt – no doubt at all – that we were going to win. And we didn't even get one goal! That'll really take some explaining to the head.'

'The old man won't need Ted's explanation,' Mark replied. 'He saw for himself that the other lot were the better team on the day.'

The chairman, with another brisk handshake and a beaming 'Hard lines, you played well,' for every recipient, handed out the medals.

As the exuberant Zeelanders, their trophy held high, set off on their lap of honour, the Hedger's players hurried to their dressing-room. To their great relief, Ted Bayley didn't put in an appearance. No one wasted much time in the showers or in getting dressed. They wanted to get away from the scene of disaster as quickly as possible, before, as Derek Vernmore put it, 'you-know-who comes in to start cutting us up for the post-mortem.' Derek, much to Mark's surprise, was taking the defeat well: he'd expected the skipper to blow his top.

Mark had arranged to meet his grandfather by the main entrance, and Jackie, who seemed in need of someone to talk to, accompanied him. In spite of the heat, Ralph Blackshaw looked as spruce as ever, not a silvery hair out of place, though he was blotting his face with a large crimson handkerchief.

'Oh dear, what a dreadful result,' he greeted them, sounding as thoroughly downcast as he looked. 'You were dreadfully unlucky, you know. That referee deserves a proper wigging from the authorities. You were well and truly robbed!'

Mark laughed. 'We wuz robbed! Oh yeah, that'll make a good epitaph.'

With so many people still milling about the main entrance, neither he nor Jackie had noticed Ted Bayley, now on the point of pushing past them. A glint in his eyes, the sports master paused.

'Glad to see that you can still laugh, Fox,' he said gratingly. 'But then the school team doesn't matter to you, does it? Well, that's all right by me because there are going to be changes next season, big changes.'

Then, without so much as a glance in Mr Blackshaw's direction, he continued on his way. Who, Mark's grandfather asked, was that? Mark told him.

'Typical, typical,' Mr Blackshaw responded fiercely. 'Just like any club manager, and I suppose that's what he's the equivalent of. When things go right they try to seize all the credit, all the glory. But when their team loses, well, it's the *team's* fault. No blame to be attached to the manager. Utter bosh! That man obviously doesn't know the first thing about psychology. He should be commiserating with his players, trying to lift them up, not uttering threats about next season.'

'Oh, forget him, Grandad,' Mark said cheerily. 'We lost and that's it. There's no point in digging graves and I couldn't care less about *next* season. I want to think about – '

'It's all right for you, Mark,' Jackie muttered. 'You've got so much to look forward to, like Switzerland. All I've got is the school team – and it looks like I'm going to be kicked out of that now. They won't drop you, will they? An England international. That's what you'll be when you get back from Switzerland.'

Before Mark could think of any reply, Mr Blackshaw put his arm round Jackie's shoulders.

'My boy,' he said gently, 'in football, nothing is certain. No one knows what the future is going to bring.'

Chapter Four

ENGLAND EXPECTS

Before they had all piled into the coach taking them out to Heathrow Airport, Terry Mercer had inquired which of them had flown previously. He looked mildly surprised when the great majority of them raised their hands.

'Just shows what an affluent age we live in,' he remarked. 'I was much older than any of you lot before anybody thought of paying for me to go up in a plane. Anyway, as most of you are such experienced jet-style travellers, I really don't need to bother with the patter about how relaxing flying is, how much there is to see in spite of being among the clouds – and that no one should try to open a window while we are up there.'

When he paused it was obviously for laughter, and there was a dutiful response that seemed to meet with his approval. With the exception of Mark, it appeared that none of the party had met the manager before, and so they didn't know quite what to expect of him. Most had already summed him up as reasonably affable, probably fair-minded but undoubtedly tough when he felt the need to be. At the assembly point he had greeted Mark pleasantly enough, saying that he was pleased to see him again and hoping that he was feeling in good form for the tour. To Mark's surprise, however, Terry Mercer hadn't made any direct reference to Mark's visit to Rowbay, when, for one match, they'd actually played together in the same team. Mark wondered whether that was a hint not to attempt to trade on familiarity. As team-mates, he'd naturally called him Terry, but he supposed that wouldn't be allowed henceforth; after all, Mercer was the equivalent of a club manager whose players would address him as Boss or Mr Mercer. So far, Mark hadn't used any name at all; he was waiting to see what the manager preferred.

'Done much flying then?' Keith Bridgeman asked Mark as they settled into adjoining seats towards the rear of the coach.

'Just the one trip to Edinburgh with my Dad. He was doing some special installations for the Post Office up there and he managed to wangle it so I could go with him. It was great, but I wish it had been Glasgow – then I'd've been able to go and watch Rangers or Celtic. What about you?'

'Flew to Paris a couple of years ago. Fantastic airport that was. It's called Charles de Gaulle and it's circular, the main building. When you're inside and you want to move up to different levels you travel on escalators – well, moving walkways actually – that are in transparent tubes. They criss-cross all over the hollow centre of the terminal. It's a bit weird seeing all the other passengers just sliding past you, or above you, or under you, and in complete silence. Like something on another planet, or maybe life

44

in the next century. Great experience, though. Makes poor old Heathrow look like last year's bus shelter!'

Mark hadn't known that, after football, travel was Keith's great passion. They had played together on many occasions, and on the same side in representative matches, and Mark had the highest regard for his friend's ability as a goalkeeper. Although rather slightly built for such a role, Bridgeman made up for lack of height with rare agility and utter fearlessness in going for the ball, however dangerous the situation in the goalmouth. He had sharp, restless eyes and never seemed to miss a trick in tactical manœuvres. If Mark had to stake his life on choosing one player to get a cap for England one day, he'd have no hesitation in picking Keith Bridgeman.

'What do you make of Terry Mercer, then?' he asked him now. He supposed that Keith would have picked up some gossip about the manager from other players, and he was right.

'Hard to tell. Seems friendly enough and he looks pretty fit to me. I hear he's terrifically ambitious. Well, that's O.K., because if he's ambitious for himself he's got to be ambitious for his squad. So that can't be bad for us, can it? If he does well, then we must be doing well.'

Mark nodded. That was certainly one way of looking at things, and it helped to balance out some of the doubts about Mercer that Albie Jones had expressed. Not for the first time, Mark wished that Albie had been picked for the tour: he was going to miss his old partner's rumbustiousness on the field and his good humour off it. He guessed that he would find himself spending most of his time in Switzerland in the company of Keith. Well, that was all right as long as Keith didn't descend into one of the moods of black depression which affected him from time to time.

'Who's that vast guy with all the fuzzy black hair?'

Mark wanted to know. 'Must be a centre-back with that sort of build.'

'Right,' nodded Keith, plainly as well-informed as usual. 'Plays for some team in the West Country, though Arsenal are supposed to be after him. Name's Eric Trowell, which is why he's known as Digger.' He grinned and added: 'I heard somebody described him as a human earth-moving machine. He should just suit Arsenal if they do get him. Anyway, I'm glad he's on our side and not the opposition. I wouldn't fancy trying to stop him charging into the box with the ball at his size-fifteen feet!'

For the remainder of the trip along the M4 and the approach to Heathrow they discussed the other players they knew in the party. Characteristically, Keith made no mention, however, of the other goalkeeper: he presumed he himself would be first choice for the team and therefore there was little point in considering someone else's claims.

Then, just before the coach pulled into the parking bay, Keith with a calculating sidelong glance at his companion, mentioned the one player who was already in the forefront of Mark's mind.

'I see the boy wonder is with us. Must say, I'm a bit surprised they picked him, however good he is. I mean, he's only a kid.'

'Mickey Hexton? No, he's not as young as he looks, Keith. In fact, he's only just about a year younger than me. Anyway, he can play a bit whatever the size of the opposition.'

Mark wasn't inclined to say much more about the player he recognised as his greatest rival. The first time they had met, Mickey had been playing for a Boys' Brigade side called Calverley Company and Mark had been in the opposing team. Mickey had been brilliant then – and brilliant every other time he'd seen him play. Fair-haired and fragile-looking, Hexton possessed a devastating body-swerve and supreme confidence in taking on any defender, skills which had earned him the nickname of The Pocket Conjuror. Mickey had never tried to compensate for his size in the company of team-mates by being over-friendly; usually he gave the impression of being rather reserved. Whenever Mark had seen him on his own, he was invariably deep in a book, often a paperback Western with a garish cover. It seemed an unlikely choice of reading matter for a boy who, in spite of frequent and sometimes severe intimidation on the pitch, had never been known to retaliate.

Mickey had been one of the last to arrive at the assembly point. On spotting Mark he'd smiled a greeting, but, probably because Mark was chatting away to Keith, hadn't gone across to have a word with him. On the coach, Mickey had a seat to himself – and was engrossed in another book.

Shepherded by Arthur Manton, the travelling physiotherapist, the players made their way from the coach to the rank of check-in desks, where they thankfully handed over their luggage and received boarding cards.

'Makes you really feel you're going, that you're actually on your way, when you get one of these,' Keith rejoiced. 'I always hate giving 'em up on the plane!'

Mark was watching the indicator board, fascinated by the rapid flickering that accompanied every announcement of flight number, destination and departure time. Both letters and numerals looked as though they'd been designed by a computer, and that seemed to be confirmed by the speed of the operation as one flight leader took off and was instantly replaced by another, with the remainder, equally swiftly, assuming new positions of precedence.

Unnoticed by Mark as he stared upwards, Mickey Hexton had drifted over to stand beside him. For some moments he was silent, sharing Mark's rapt interest. Then, with a sense of simple joy that none of the other players would have expressed even had they felt it, he remarked: 'It's very thrilling, isn't it?'

'Oh, er, hello, Mickey. Yeah, great.'

'That's us, isn't it, up there? The Swissair to Zurich?'

'That's it! No turning back now. We're practically on our way.'

At that moment, Terry Mercer signalled, with a flourish of his passport, that his squad should follow him to the departure lounge. The physio, whose neatly-trimmed white hair was a fair indication of his age, had plainly been allotted the task of ensuring that at no stage of the tour was the party going to be held up by stragglers. Already some of the players were referring to him as Doc. He appeared not to mind.

'I'm very glad you're with us, Mark,' said Mickey, falling in to step with him. 'But I knew you would be. They couldn't leave you out.'

'Oh? Well, I was pretty stunned to get the invitation. I didn't know anything about the tour until I got that letter.' Mark was not used to receiving personal compliments from fellow players. It was all the harder to accept when it came from someone he regarded as the greatest threat to his own chances of achieving maximum success as an England Junior.

'What do you think of the manager?' he asked Mickey.

'Oh, he seems quite nice. Quite friendly, really. He told me I'd have to stand up for myself. But I know that. I always have to stand up for myself. Because I'm small they think they can get away with anything.'

'Well, from what I've seen of you, you manage O.K. Anyway, the Continentals don't go in much for the physical stuff. They rely on ball skills, long passes, positioning, the classy stuff. We'll have to match that.'

He felt he was telling Mickey something the younger

48

boy knew well enough already, but it was plain that Mickey was glad to have his company and Mark wondered whether he was going to be stuck with him for the entire trip. Keith, he noticed, was absorbed by the contents of the display cases of duty-free goods: Mark would have preferred to join him but he couldn't just get up and walk away from Mickey. So he found himself talking about his grandfather, Ralph Blackshaw, who had strong opinions about foreign sides. We used to beat 'em like clockwork in my day, he would say, relishing the memory. Continentals couldn't cope with our teamwork and our speed, we always had the edge in speed. They weren't so hot at heading or shooting. No, we could show them a thing or two at any time. Don't see why it should be any different today.

Mark, who knew that the balance of football power had shifted considerably in recent years, had remarked to his grandfather that foreign teams now beat England with the same regularity of clockwork. And weren't the Swiss supposed to be the world's best at making clocks? Aye, his grandfather had grinned, springing an old joke, they were – cuckoo clocks!

Mickey laughed at this story, and said he was looking forward to Switzerland because he'd never been abroad and hadn't dreamed he'd get the chance so soon. But he hoped to put the experience to good use, as, one day, he intended to play for a foreign club.

Before Mark could make any response to that unexpected revelation, there was a general movement among the players. Messrs Mercer and Manton were on their feet, gathering the boys around them. Their flight departure had been announced.

'Well, this is it,' murmured Mickey, eyes gleaming. 'Switzerland, here we come!'

As they ascended the steps into the Swissair Boeing, it

was Tommy Archbold, the tall Merseyside striker, who spotted the photographers on the tarmac, apparently taking farewell pictures of the squad. Pausing, he clasped his hands above his head and chanted: 'Cham-pions, champions!'

'All right, Tommy, all right, that'll do. Cut out the exhibition stuff,' Terry Mercer called out to him from below. 'We haven't played a match yet, let alone won anything.'

Tommy continued on his way, ducking his head to enter the aircraft. But not before he'd commented to the player nearest to him: 'There y'are, wack. That's managers for you. Not a shred of confidence in their own team!'

Mark, who was just behind him, grinned to himself. He could imagine what Mercer's response would have been had he heard that. Known to team-mates and opponents alike as Tearaway Tommy, Archbold could be guaranteed to enliven the scene when he was around.

Mickey had managed to get a seat next to a window and was totally absorbed in all that was going on in and around the aircraft. Keith, sitting beside Mark, was already talking about football again and England's prospects of winning their mini-World Cup. His great hope was that several First Division club managers would be present 'with registration forms at the ready to sign up all the talent'. Mark was only half-listening. An aeroplane's take-off was a bit like the moments before kick-off in a vital match: a time of nervousness and uncertainty about the future. He rather envied both Keith's detachment and Mickey's quiet enthusiasm for new sensations.

Once they were airborne, however, he relaxed and much enjoyed the meal that was served. To follow the steak and peas there was some of the most delicious cheese he'd ever tasted and milk chocolate and apple juice. In front of them, Tommy Archbold could be heard proclaiming that 'This is the life, lads! Luxury and all for free.'

'The Swiss make the world's best chocolate, you know,' Mickey observed. 'And cheese as well, I think. It's funny, really, but everyone seems to think that all they make is cuckoo clocks,' he added to Mark's chagrin.

'Yeah, but they don't go in much for making football teams, do they?' said Keith.

'Oh, I don't know about that, Keith,' replied Mickey, looking very serious. 'They have more players than in the whole of Brazil, and yet Switzerland's only a small country. Actually, they have exactly as many as Scotland. And their Association was formed way back in 1895, years ahead of the big South American countries and even West Germany. I've been reading up all the records and statistics, you see.'

'Yeah, well it's like I said, they haven't got very far, have they,' Keith retaliated, refusing to concede any point at all. 'We'll have a walk-over when we play Switzerland. When England turn on the heat the Swiss will melt like their own milk chocolate!'

As the plane began its descent to Zurich, Mickey leaned across to Mark and asked in a confidential tone: 'Will the Customs Officers have to search us all? You know, personally, our clothes and things?'

Mark was puzzled. 'Well, I don't think so, Mickey. I mean, don't they usually search you when you get back to England?'

Keith, who'd overheard, seized on the idea that Mickey was trying to do some smuggling. He wanted to know what he'd got in his luggage and tried to make a joke that it was a secret weapon for defeating the opposition or possibly high-powered drugs to provide super-energy. Mickey looked distinctly embarrassed and wouldn't say what he was carrying. Keith persisted in trying to find out

51

what it was and was still at it when they left the plane. Mark had to nudge him in the ribs and tell him to forget it.

In fact, none of the Swiss officials took any interest at all in the players' papers or belongings. They seemed pleased to see the Union Jack on so many holdalls and one said: 'We hope you play well in your matches. We admire the English players.'

'That's right, wack,' Tommy Archbold responded. 'We're the greatest. Come and watch us. You'll learn a lot!'

The official laughed. Clearly he understood a youngster of Tommy's character. To the boys' delighted surprise he even stepped out from behind his desk and mimed the action of taking a penalty kick. They cheered his effort and told him he'd scored. His smile behind his rimless spectacles was enormous.

There was a slight delay before they headed for their coach, and Mark noticed that a man in a very pale blue lightweight jacket and a black, peaked cap was taking a close interest in the party. He pointed him out to Keith.

'Do you think he's a secret agent – or a German football scout? Looks as if he's sizing us up.'

Keith glanced across at the man, and then guffawed. 'I reckon he's an undercover Customs officer. Checking up on smugglers. Mickey, you'd better confess now and hand the stuff over or you'll finish up in a Swiss prison. Handcuffed to an iron ring in the deepest, darkest cellar!'

Mickey muttered something inaudible, but, as if taking the threat seriously, turned away. The odd thing was, the agent *did* seem to be watching Mickey – or so it appeared to Mark. Then he dismissed the idea as a far-fetched coincidence.

The squad had been hoping that one of the other teams, perhaps West Germany or Holland, might arrived at the airport at the same time, but there was no sign of them. So

52

the first confrontation was probably going to take place on the pitch after all. As far as they knew, the draw for the order of play hadn't been made yet, and so they didn't know who their first opponents would be. Most hoped it would be Switzerland, because, as Keith had already stated, they surely would be the weakest side. Mickey, for one, took the opposite view: if England played and defeated the toughest opposition first, then they'd be set up for the rest of the tournament in terms of confidence. Mark agreed with him.

Doc Manton started rounding them up again, and ushered them towards the exit. Behind the taxi rank, a luxurious-looking yellow and green coach was waiting. Its entire roof appeared to be made of glass.

Terry Mercer had already told the players that they would be staying in a training college just outside the city and would have the use of two or three football pitches for practice purposes. Rooms would be allocated when he and Mr Manton had had the opportunity of inspecting the accommodation.

The ride through the centre of the city brought a variety of comments from the boys, but it was one from Tommy Archbold that caused the greatest laugh.

'Place reminds me of Liverpool, lads,' he said, drawing, as no doubt he expected, a reaction of total disbelief. 'Just one difference, though. In Liverpool there's a pub on every corner, here, there's a bank on every corner!'

That looked to be true. Mickey tried to keep count of all the different banks they passed but soon gave it up as an impossible task.

At last the coach slowed down and then swung left between tall, wrought-iron gates into a gravelled drive.

The manager, who'd been seated at the front by the driver, stood up and turned to face them. Conversation died away immediately.

'Right, boys, I want your attention,' he announced solemnly. 'The fun part of the trip is over – for the time being, anyway. As soon as we've settled in here I want you all down on the practice ground immediately, in your playing kit. We're here to work and there's no time to be wasted. I came to Switzerland to win – and so did you. Now, and I mean now, we're going to set about converting ambition into reality.'

Chapter Five

A SHOCK FOR MARK

By the middle of the following morning, many of the players were feeling completely worn out. For the second time in well under twenty-four hours, Terry Mercer had put them through a vigorous training session on the College practice pitches. With Doc Manton acting as a hawk-eyed first lieutenant, none of them had managed more than a few moments' respite from ball work, sprinting exercises, a complicated and punishing series of gymnastic endeavours, and, to the amazement from most of the boys, a short spell of what the manager called 'soccer on horse-back'.

'This'll sort out the weaklings, the ones who haven't bothered to strengthen *all* the muscles in the body,' he told them with a rare grin. He was wearing black shorts and a bright yellow tee-shirt and carried a whistle on a long lanyard looped round his neck. 'Soccer is a game of strength as well as skill, remember. I want players in my team who'll last the full eighty minutes without flagging. Endurance can be just as important as ability.'

He had their rapt attention as he explained how the competition was to be played. Teams would consist of three players, each of whom would carry another player on his shoulders. Consternation or utter disbelief was immediately reflected on the face of every boy in the squad. Those with the sharpest minds quickly glanced round at team-mates, assessing which would be the lightest to have to support. Inevitably, most settled on Mickey Hextons, who obviously weighed less than anyone else.

As if totally unaware that this covert selection procedure was taking place as he spoke, Mercer defined the playing area by marching briskly along the perimeter of a zone measuring approximately fifteen metres by sixteen metres.

'Each team defends its own goal-line, team A on the left, team B on the right,' he continued. 'You score by dribbling the ball over your opponents' line. *Dribbling*, I said. No shooting. In other words, you've got to work the ball over the line to score. O.K.? You try to win the ball in the usual way, by dispossessing opponents by tackling or intercepting passes. No rough stuff from the players being carried, by the way – they just sit there and keep their balance. Nothing else. When a team scores, possession is automatically awarded to the other side.'

He paused, perhaps in expectation of receiving questions, but none was forthcoming.

'Now, I know you're all thinking of picking a lightweight to carry but that isn't on – *I* will pick the pairs on the basis of equal sizes. Which means, Mickey, that you'll sit this one out. You've done enough this morning, anyway.'

Mickey, uncertain whether to be relieved or disappointed, just nodded. He caught Mark's eye and got a sympathetic smile. Mark was thinking that such a game as this was typical of Terry Mercer's training routines. When he'd been at Rowbay, the players there had been deployed in similar, though possibly less demanding exercises that Terry had devised and supervised.

'In any case,' the manager concluded, 'after one minute's play each pair will change over, so the one who's been in-active will then be doing the carrying. I'm sure I don't need to tell you that this game is designed to develop the leg muscles. It'll teach you to *stand* the pace, if you see what I mean!'

Only Doc Manton seemed to appreciate the joke. The laughter from the players sounded distinctly hollow. The majority thought they'd done quite enough work already that morning, to say nothing of the previous afternoon's work-out.

Mark was paired with David Redmile, the boy who was generally expected to be given the captaincy of the first team Mercer chose for the tournament. They'd first met when playing on opposing sides in London, and Mark had a good deal of respect for David's skills as a hard-tackling full-back, with a surprising turn of speed for a defender.

'Don't think much of this carry-on,' muttered Redmile. 'He's flogging us to death. We'll be whacked before we ever get round to playing a real game.'

Dire thoughts of what they were all in for gave way to some hilarity, however, when it was realised that Tommy Archbold was trying to persuade someone to give him a hand in climbing on to Digger Trowell's shoulders. As Keith Bridgeman remarked, that combination was going to look like a mobile skyscraper. Tommy, though, seemed to be enjoying the experience.

'Makes a change to be carried *by* a centre-half,' he declared. 'They're usually falling all over me.'

Then, as if wielding a whip, he proceeded to lash his

mount into action. Obediently, Digger cantered over to the playing area, apparently supporting his rider with effortless ease.

Mark, trying to ignore the burden on his shoulders, was thankful that the Archbold–Trowell combination was on his side; he'd have hated to try and take the ball off them. Indeed, Tommy was in the mood to make the most of the situation and was trying to strike bets with opponents that he would score at least one goal. Nobody was prepared to take him on.

'Give us the ball when you get it, wack,' he said to Mark. 'We'll knock that lot over with no trouble.'

In fact, it was Tommy who first gained control of the ball after Mercer had rolled it between the lines of opponents to set the game in motion. For, in the scramble for possession, the ball suddenly ricocheted vertically off someone's knee-cap and Tommy, leaning forward precariously, grabbed it with both hands and then tried to urge Digger into a trot.

Fiercely, Terry Mercer blew for an infringement. Spectators and the rest of the players had treated the incident as a joke but the manager wasn't at all amused.

'Training is a *serious* business, not a comedy show, Tommy,' he told the offender. He ran a hand through his crinkly ginger hair and then announced that he was awarding a goal to the other side as the punishment for the handling offence. He would re-start the game by again rolling the ball between the two ranks.

'That's not fair, Boss!' Tommy protested. 'You just said that if one side scores the other side gets possession. You can't change the flaming rules in the first minute!'

The manager was unmoved by that appeal. 'I'm not changing the rules. Just enforcing them. Now let's get on with the game.'

This time it was Mark who succeeded in controlling the

ball, but as he tried to turn with it, the weight on his shoulders very nearly caused him to lose his balance. David, swaying first one way and then the other, yelled in alarm that he was falling. Mark halted – and Kevin Bonnell, his nearest opponent, confidently took the ball away from him, seemingly unhampered by his rider. Although moving at not much more than snail's pace, Kevin made good progress towards the goal-line.

'Well done, Kevin, that's the way,' Mercer urged.

'Hey, that's not on!' Tommy roared at the manager. 'You're supposed to be neutral.'

That criticism was ignored. Digger, however, strode heavily but unstoppably into Kevin's path like a bulldozer. As Kevin tried to weave past him Digger stuck out a toe and nudged the ball towards Mark.

With what, under other circumstances, would have been a neat sidestep – but which felt and looked cumbersome – Mark evaded the challenge of an opposing pair and headed for the goal-line.

'Keep going, Mark,' David urged. Unfortunately, in his excitement he grabbed handfuls of Mark's hair. The pain was as severe as it was sudden. Mark stumbled, put his foot on the ball – and crashed to the ground with David landing on top of him. From the watchers, there was a derisive cheer.

'*You'll* never win the Grand National,' Tommy bellowed. 'Bloody fools! We had a certain goal there. Come on, get up and get on with the game!'

Mark felt as if he'd been crushed by a steam-roller. He took his time in getting to his feet, fearful that he'd damaged something that would put him out of action for the tournament. Under his breath, when he got it back, he heaped curses on Terry Mercer. It was absolute stupidity to organise a game with so many built-in risks as this one. But, rather to his own surprise, he found that he was unhurt; and David was already trying to resume his seat.

'All right?' inquired the manager as they re-entered the play.

'Oh, sure, great, just great,' Mark replied with unveiled sarcasm.

Once again, Digger had secured possession and was now lumbering towards the line with the eager Tommy jogging up and down on his shoulders. Digger was within a couple of strides of scoring the equaliser when the referee halted him, and everyone else, with a blast of the whistle.

Tommy was furious. 'What the hell's that for, ref?'

'Change-over – one minute is up,' was the calm reply. 'Right, your turn to be the horse, Tommy.'

Eager as ever to show off his strength, Tommy swiftly hoisted Digger on to his shoulders and was impatient for everyone else to be as well organised. Then, the instant the whistle blew for the game to continue, he barged forward and swept the ball over the line. Jubilantly he flung his arms in the air and very nearly knocked his partner to the ground.

Terry Mercer signalled his approval. In spite of their minor clashes, which had so far been fairly good-tempered, he appeared to have formed a high opinion of Tearaway Tommy. He liked the Merseysider's enthusiasm and whole-hearted endeavour – and, naturally, his physical prowess, because that proved that Tommy was fit.

Although being carried was less exhausting than acting as the horse, Mark felt distinctly insecure on David Red-mile's shoulders; every time his partner made a move-ment Mark was sure he was going to fall off. He found he couldn't care less about winning the contest; all that mattered was avoiding injury. As soon as this training session was over, Terry Mercer was likely to announce the team to play in the first match the following afternoon.

England had been drawn against Holland in the opening game. The general opinion of the squad was that the Dutch side would provide neither the hardest nor the easiest opposition. Nonetheless, it was felt that Mercer had no option but to select what he considered to be his strongest team. After all, it would be a dreadful blow to any team's morale to lose the first match.

David was not exerting himself in the horseback game and the Boss spotted that.

'Get on with it, David,' he ordered sharply. 'You haven't done enough yet to be tired. We're playing on for the deciding goal.'

Mark heard his mount utter some imprecation before trying to raise a gallop. If Redmile was being criticised openly, that could mean that he wasn't going to be picked as captain.

There really wasn't much doubt about how the game was going to end. When David, summoning up all his remaining energy, collected the ball, he carefully rounded an opponent before stabbing an accurate pass to Tommy. As he did so he tilted dangerously over to the left and Mark felt himself to be on the point of falling again; somehow, though, David managed to steady himself and the combination remained upright. Tommy, meanwhile, had pounded towards the goal-line with Digger displaying a perfect sense of balance. Then, as he scored, Tommy tried to exercise a skip of success, tripped over his own feet and tumbled in a heap. Digger, imitating a steeplechase jockey, contrived to land on his shoulder and roll over and over before getting to his feet, unscathed.

Tommy lay flat out on his back, seemingly out cold. The laughter that had greeted his antics died away. With an expression of real alarm, Doc Manton hurried forward. Terry, whistle at his lips but unblown, remained motionless.

Then, to the Boss's undisguised relief, Tommy, just as Manton was about to kneel beside him, athletically somersaulted to his feet and waved his arms in the air.

'We are the Champions!' he yelled. 'Who hit the winner? Arch-bold, Arch-bold!'

Dutifully, the rest of the players gave him the applause he was seeking.

'O.K., lads, time for a rest now,' Mercer told them. 'Let's get over by the pool. Then you can have a swim to cool off – *after* I've given you the news you've all been waiting for.'

'Oh great, the suspense has been killing me,' said Tommy, still in his theatrical mood.

'Yeah, you did your best to kill *me* just now, Archbold,' Digger told him, aiming a mock piledriver at the Liverpool striker.

The players spread themselves on the grassed bank in front of the kidney-shaped swimming pool, its flawlessly-clean water as blue as the sky. Although it wasn't quite as warm as it had been when they left England, they were all eager to plunge in after their strenuous exertions. Mark's legs were still aching, and he reckoned that Redmile was even more solidly built than he looked. He was thankful that the Londoner wasn't going to be in the Dutch line-up.

'Before I announce the names of the players for our first match against Holland, there's one thing I want to make clear to you all,' Mercer began formally as he stood in front of them. 'As I said when we arrived, we're here to win, not simply to give a good account of ourselves and be admired for our sportsmanship. English football has been going through a bad spell, and, in international terms, we've lost some of our old prestige. We need to start winning again, to start looking really good again.' Mercer paused for a moment.

'Some of you may think that because we're a junior side, and a long way from home, people in England won't be much interested in what we do, or don't do. That couldn't be further from the truth. These matches, the whole tournament, will get press coverage. I know of at least two journalists from national papers in London who are coming out here – and there will be reports going out from the international press agencies as well. I'm sure I don't have to tell you, either, that some club managers will be present – they'll be here to size up the quality of this squad as well as to see what the foreigners can produce. So we want to give them a fillip by demonstrating that English football has a great future. A *great* future.'

Behind Mercer's shoulder, Doc Manton was nodding vigorously. None of the players was paying any attention to him at that moment. Each was waiting expectantly to hear his own name mentioned. But Terry Mercer still hadn't completed his preamble.

'There's one additional point I must make. You've probably heard that it's the usual policy with a tour party for every player to be given a game at some stage. But that won't necessarily happen on this tour – or in this tournament, rather. As I've said, I'm here to win, so I must play the *best* team every time.' The manager looked around his squad.

'That may seem harsh to anyone who finds himself left out of the side, but if you think about it from the *team's* viewpoint rather than the individual's, then you'll see it makes sense. Of course, injuries and loss of form can play havoc with any manager's plans, so those who are omitted from the first side mustn't assume that they're *never* going to get a game.'

Mark had crossed his fingers fiercely behind his back as the manager went on, 'I'm telling you all this, lads, because I believe in being honest with every player. I don't believe in dealing in – well – crafty deceptions. Honesty is the vital ingredient in a relationship between a manager and his players. You must feel that you can trust me, and I must be able to trust you. O.K., now I've got that off my chest, I'll give you the news you've been waiting for. The team to play Holland tomorrow will be: Bridgeman; Redmile, the captain, Willett, Trowell and Kennan; the midfield three, Forster, Wade and Hilton; strikers, Bonnell, Archbold and Hexton. Substitute, Fox.'

Mark felt stunned. Even though he'd never considered himself a certainty for selection, he'd been fairly confident of a place. But what really staggered him was that Mickey Hexton had been chosen. For, if Terry Mercer meant what he said, Mickey, the player Mark regarded as his chief rival, would be playing in every match. Unless, of course, he was unable to cope with the physical aspects of what surely would be an unrelentingly tough competition. Had Mickey the strength to stand up to crushing tackles and the non-stop buffeting that was the lot of every striker in and around the box?

As sub, Mark was bound to be next in line for a game; on the other hand, if Mercer was determined on an all-out attacking policy, then Mark was the *only* choice for that role. The other three players left out were the reserve goalie, an out-and-out back-four defender and a midfield specialist. The only striker omitted was Mark. So being sub was no consolation at all.

He couldn't help wondering whether he'd done something to upset the Boss. When they'd played together at Rowbay, Mark had scored after a fine solo run and Terry himself had described the goal as a cracker. Terry was a defender – he'd played as centre-back and sweeper – and one of his players at Rowbay had summed him up by saying that he was a hard man, on and off the field. Whether he was fair-minded was another matter. Mark felt that, if

63

only on the basis of his performance at Rowbay, he should have been picked for the Holland match; but perhaps, he reflected, Mercer was deliberately not allowing himself to be influenced by past events. In any case, he admitted to himself, it was quite possible that Terry had completely forgotten that game at Rowbay. Not for the first time since leaving England, Mark wished that Albie Jones were present to offer some pertinent advice as well as sympathy.

There was no doubting who was the happiest member of the squad. Mickey Hexton was overjoyed. It was evident from his reaction that he hadn't imagined that he would be in the team.

'Fantastic, fantastic,' he was saying, over and over again. 'I just can't believe it. I think I must be dreaming. To be picked for England . . .'

David Redmile had the answer to that. 'Then we'll have to wake you up, Mickey. Anyway, a new international always has to be properly baptised, you know.'

He exchanged a knowing look with his fellow defender and long-time friend, Jimmy Kennan, and, as one, they swooped on Mickey. Before the blond-haired youngster had realised what was happening they had lifted him bodily and were heading for the edge of the pool.

'Oh no, no, please!' Mickey protested. 'I'll get my kit all soaked. Don't do that, David.'

To his own surprise they immediately put him down, but without releasing their hold on him. Then, with a grinning Tommy Archbold coming forward to assist, they tugged his shirt over his head, slipped his boots and socks off and started to pull his shorts down.

'Oh, no, no,' Mickey wailed again. 'You can't – '

Mickey was struggling furiously but was powerless to prevent three of his strongest team-mates succeeding in their aims. In any case, they were being cheered on by other members of the squad who were now in the mood

64

to enjoy a bit of fun. Even the Boss was smiling in genial fashion and plainly was not going to interfere; he was pleased to see such a good spirit in the party.

It was only when they'd stripped him completely that they saw that Mickey was wearing a curious form of belt that looked to be made of a kind of webbing material. It was fastened round the upper part of his right thigh. Its presence so astonished Tommy and David that they relaxed their hold on their victim. Mickey seized his chance to escape. Without so much as a glance at his discarded kit he fled over the bank and across the lawn and disappeared inside the College building.

The cheers that accompanied his flight were mostly half-hearted, however. Several of the boys had noted how distraught Mickey appeared to be. At the same time, they couldn't help speculating on the reason for such a belt: for it certainly wasn't a new form of bandage or any other kind of support.

'O.K., lads, that's enough of the fooling for now,' Terry called. 'High jinks are fine, they're part of every soccer squad you'll ever meet. Just as long as no one suffers any injury. Remember that Mickey's not quite as tough as the rest of you. So don't give him a hard time because he's the youngest. Anyway, those who want a swim, now's your chance.'

Terry Mercer approached his new substitute. 'Mark, you're one of Mickey's room-mates. Better take his kit up to him and see he's O.K. If I go up there now he'll probably think I'm prying into his private life. I can have a word with him later. But if he's really worried about something, Mark, come and tell me.'

Mark, rather surprised by the request, silently gathered up Mickey's gear and slowly made his way into the College while the rest of his team-mates plunged or slid into the pool. It crossed his mind as he climbed the wide,

65

manorial-style staircase, that Terry Mercer just might want to get him out of the way for some reason. Did he want to talk privately to the team without risk of being overheard by the sub? 'I must be going bonkers,' he told himself. 'At this rate I'll go mad with a persecution complex.' For, now that he really thought about things, it was obvious that if the Boss had wanted to confer secretly with his chosen team he wouldn't have allowed them to split up and enjoy a swimming session. All the same, he couldn't help feeling disgruntled. If the same situation had arisen at a League club, he'd have been slapping in a transfer request by now.

In the eyes of most of the occupants, the rooms allotted to the players were in the luxury class: comfortable divan beds of the studio-couch kind; separate, capacious wardrobes with enough drawers and shelves to accommodate an outfitter's private stock; wall lights, and reading lights over each bed; wood-block polished floors; balconied windows; and, best of all, a private bathroom to every room. The majority of the rooms were for two people but, as the three youngest players in the party, Mark was sharing with Keith Bridgeman and Mickey.

Mickey was lying face down on his own bed. He hadn't bothered to get dressed again and the web belt was still in place. Carefully placing the clothes on a chair, Mark perched on the edge of Mickey's bed and put his hand gently on his shoulder.

'Feeling O.K. now, Mick?' he asked softly.

Mickey's response was muffled by the pillow. It was impossible to tell what he said. Mark hoped that he wasn't crying; that would be embarrassing for both of them.

'Look, it wasn't important, nothing to get steamed up about,' he said. 'You must know that sort of thing happens at every club – players are always taking the mickey out of somebody, ducking them in the bath or pinching their

66

pants, all that sort of caper. It gets rid of the tensions – that's what one coach I know used to say.'

Suddenly, unexpectedly, Mickey rolled over on his back. To Mark's surprise, Mickey's eyes were neither red nor blurred. His gaze was as clear as it was steady – and cold.

'Maybe that's how it seems to you, Mark, but I know different. Maybe it starts as a joke but it finishes up as bullying. Picking on the smallest and making him suffer.'

Mark stared back at him disbelievingly. 'Come off it, Mickey! Nobody wants to bully you. The lads here aren't like that.'

'Have you ever been bullied, Mark? Really had your life made a misery, so that you just want to curl up and hide down a deep hole and never come out again? Hated, really *hated*, your tormentors and wished they were dead? Have you, Mark?'

'Er, no, never. No, of course not.'

'I thought not,' Mickey went on in a very level tone. 'You're big enough to take care of yourself. You're tall and pretty solidly-built so you don't get that sort of treatment. But it happens to me all the time where I live. The other kids pick on me because I'm cleverer than they are, I can do most things better than they can. They don't like the idea that someone smaller than them can be the best at anything – and because I get extra privileges, like this trip to Switzerland, for being good at football, it makes them madder still. They're just like terrorists. And I'm their favourite victim.'

'But why can't you just keep out of their way? I mean, you're pretty fast on your feet even if you are small. Surely you could out-distance them if you really set your mind to it?'

'I can run faster than them, but there's nowhere to run to. You see, they all live in the same place as me.'

'At your home . . . ?'

67

Mark's bewilderment was so great that, for the first time since he'd returned to the bedroom, Mickey smiled. He had relaxed enough to clasp his hands behind his head.

'Not *my* home, Mark, *a* home – a home with a capital H. A home for orphans. I don't have any parents, you see. Well, I have a father – or I think I do – but no one knows where he is.'

He paused as if to give Mark the chance to say something. But Mark didn't know what to say. Any expression of sympathy he could utter would be totally inadequate, he realised.

'He ran away with another woman just after I was born,' Mickey continued. 'He just vanished. But I think he went to Australia. I don't know why, really, but I just have a feeling that's where he is. One day I'll meet him. I don't know how or why but I think it'll happen. Anyway, after he'd gone, my mother just kept going on her own. Then she got ill and died. Some mysterious disease. I was eight then and I had to go into a home because there was no one to look after me. I don't have any aunts or uncles or anyone like that – and my grandparents were dead as well.'

Mark shook his head. 'That's terrible, Mickey. Honestly, I'd no idea, no idea at all that you, well, didn't have a normal life like the rest of us.'

'Oh, that's all right. I don't go on about it, you know. No point. I mean, it sounds like the original hard luck story, doesn't it? But it's not so bad really. It's just the bullying that's hard to take. Sometimes, when they're in the mood, they even wake me up in the middle of the night and give me the cold bath treatment. I really hate that. They think it's a huge joke because they reckon all pro footballers get the cold bath treatment after a match so they think I should be in training for it. It's all because they're jealous of the way I can play – none of them

68

would get into the local works' side, even as a sub! You see, that's why I couldn't take it out there this afternoon by the swimming pool. It was like a bad dream – the whole rotten trick happening again just when I thought I'd got away from it for a whole week. I could have put up with anything else – but not that.'

A feeling of embarrassment was now dominating Mark's reactions. He wished that Mickey hadn't told him so much. He wished fervently that Redmile and Kennan hadn't acted so stupidly and thus precipitated all these confidences. He still wished he could do something that would help Mickey but that, he sensed, was impossible.

'Thanks for listening, Mark,' said Mickey with obvious sincerity. He sat up and reached for his clothes. 'I've never been able to tell anybody all that before. I just sort of, well, kept it buttoned up. But I wanted you to know why I ran away like that from the swimming pool.'

'Er, what's that belt thing you've got strapped to your leg, Mickey?' asked Mark, thankful he'd thought of a way of changing the subject. 'We all thought that was the reason you ran – er, you came back up here.'

'A money belt. I made it myself. It's my hobby at the Home, making things out of leather and webbing. It's something you can do on your own – and nobody else is interested. I had to have something to conceal my spending money in, you see, so I invented this belt. It hasn't any metal on it so I knew I'd be able to pass the airport security system unless they gave everybody a personal body search. That was the only thing that worried me.'

'Oh, I see. Yeah, good idea, Mickey. Look, I'd better get back to the Boss and tell him everything's O.K. now. O.K.?'

'Yes, all right. I'll be down as soon as I've got dressed. Oh, just one thing, Mark: please don't tell the other players what I've told you, about being an orphan, I mean. If you do, they'll start joking about it sooner or later. People always do.'

'Don't worry, Mickey. I shan't tell 'em anything they don't need to know – and they certainly don't need to know that. Anyway, they'll all be thinking about the Holland match.'

As he made his way back to the squad it suddenly occurred to Mark that, during the time he was with Mickey, not once had he thought about his own predicament.

Chapter Six

THE DUTCH MASTERS

Mark couldn't remember the last time he'd sat on the subs' bench. Well, not at the start of a match, anyway. He'd been there after being pulled off late in a game because of injury, or for tactical reasons. This was a particularly hard bench and he was shifting about, trying to find a comfortable spot. Doc Manton, on his immediate left, seemed to have the same problem, but Terry Mercer, at the far end, wasn't moving a centimetre; at the moment the Boss looked as impassive as a town hall statue. Perhaps, Mark reflected, Terry wanted to give everyone, including the opposition, the impression that he wasn't worried about a single thing. He knew his team were going to win comfortably and so he was simply waiting for them to get on with it.

Firecrackers were exploding as the teams limbered up. The stadium was far from being full, but the crowd was still a good one; doubtless it would be a capacity attendance the following day, when the host nation, Switzerland, played West Germany. Mark kept looking over his shoulder and into the stands behind him, hoping to catch a glimpse of the famous English club managers who might be present. He was wondering whether Athletic's manager was among them. If so, the club's present interest in Mark Fox was bound to suffer a very sharp decline. The very fact that he hadn't been picked to play in the first match would indicate to them that Terry Mercer had little confidence in his ability. In the circumstances, Athletic might well switch their attention to other players such as Mickey Hexton or Billy Hilton. Mark could find himself out in the cold for years. He shivered at the prospect.

Of course, there was still a chance that he would get into the game. Any player could be injured and taken off – or someone could be blotted out of the game. Mark didn't really want to consider either possibility. He was as keen as everyone else in the squad for England to do well, to win handsomely and make progress in the tournament. If the side failed in the first two matches they would be eliminated from the competition, and then the decision might be made for them to make an early return home.

There was a sudden burst of applause from behind the England goal as Tommy Archbold hit a ferocious shot into the roof of the net as the shooting-in practice continued. Mickey made some remark which caused Tommy to laugh and clap him on the back; in comic fashion Mickey sagged at the knees as if the blow, friendly enough though it was, had been powerful enough to knock him over. Mickey had quickly recovered from his distress of the previous day and the rest of the boys had been treating him in a more affectionate manner, though without overdoing it. Mark wondered whether Terry Mercer had confided in them about Mickey's circumstances; after all, he was sure to know most of the details of Mickey's back-

71

ground, and, as tour manager, he was officially standing in for each player's parents or guardian. But so far no one had mentioned the subject, not even Keith Bridgeman, their room-mate.

Mark guessed that his best hope of getting on to the field was as the replacement for Mickey, who, if he played flat out from the start, would conceivably tire towards the end of the game. Even if the blond pocket conjuror were in truly dazzling form, the Boss might still pull him off, if only to conserve Mickey's energies for future matches. Mark grimaced. He didn't want to take Mickey's place. The boy had had enough rotten luck to last a lifetime as it was. All the same . . .

'They look a lively lot,' observed Doc Manton, nodding in the direction of the orange-shirted Holland team. 'Artistic, too, I'll bet. If they win, the press'll be labelling them the new Dutch masters, I reckon.'

Mark made no comment. The 'Dutch masters' description had been just about the most-quoted cliché in international football ever since the 1974 World Cup Final, and Mark had been wondering who'd be the first to use it on this tour.

'But they're not going to win, Arthur, are they?' Terry Mercer said in a reproving tone. 'I can't imagine how *you* could imagine we'll lose. We haven't come all this distance to be beaten in our first match.'

Mark had difficulty in stifling a laugh at that mild reprimand. He had seen enough of Terry Mercer at Rowbay and in Zurich to know that the Boss didn't have much of a sense of humour. Doc Manton's eyes began an exaggerated sweep of the stadium, and then, for a few moments, focused on the powder-blue sky. It was an ideal day for football: scarcely a breath of wind, a gentle sun and a firm surface. The emerald turf looked in perfect condition. It would certainly suit a player with pace who possessed real skill on the ball. Someone like himself, Mark couldn't help reflecting. On the other hand, had it been a drenching day with a morass of a pitch, Mickey Hexton would probably have tired quite quickly.

The referee, a Frenchman, had called the captains together, and, after they'd exchanged national pennants and shaken hands several times for the benefit of press photographers, he spun a coin. David Redmile appeared to have called correctly for, with no advantage in choice of ends, it was England who kicked off.

Almost immediately, Mickey was in action. Digger, having received the ball from Kevin Bonnell, slung a long pass out to the left flank. Well aware that Hexton hadn't the height to jump high for the ball, he had skilfully kept it low. Mickey, moving in-field sharply, killed the ball on his thigh, and, turning with it in the same movement, rounded his nearest opponent and started to run. It was a most accomplished piece of ball play and instantly a buzz of appreciation and excitement went round the ground. Mark bit his lip. Already Mickey was demonstrating exactly the sort of skills that Mark himself possessed.

The Dutch defenders were funnelling back as Mickey ran at them. For the moment they were rather more concerned by the threat of Tommy Archbold, boring into the danger zone with his customary belligerence. No one had yet attempted to dispossess Mickey. They must have suspected that, because he was of such slight build, even an ordinary tackle on him could look to the referee like a bulldozer dealing with a sapling.

Then Mickey, hardly seeming to glance up at all, suddenly swung his left-foot and lofted the ball to the far right. It was a beautifully-judged pass to Kevin Bonnell, who was running wide. Kevin had the reputation of being a lazy player when he wasn't directly involved in the action. Sometimes he could appear to be not very interested in the proceedings at all until the ball reached him in or around the penalty area. There, however, he was deadly: the arch-opportunist who could create a goal-scoring chance out of virtually nothing.

Now he took the ball on for a few paces, showed it to his challenger, deftly cut past him on the inside and then chipped it to the back of the box. He aimed it, not at Tommy Archbold, that would have been too obvious, but at Digger Trowell, who was charging forward at a great rate.

Suddenly, Digger's Afro hairstyle seemed to be suspended high above everyone else's head. He had timed his jump perfectly and, connecting fiercely with the ball, sent it goalwards. The Dutch keeper was a couple of metres off his line, but, luckily for him, he was in the line of fire. With a fine leap, he managed to get the tips of his fingers to the ball and divert it over the bar.

It was an exhilarating start for England and even Terry Mercer managed to display the glimmer of a smile.

'Good ball from young Hexton to start that movement,' said Doc Manton. 'He's a really gifted player, that lad.'

There was a renewed hum of expectancy as Billy Hilton went over to take the corner kick. Billy, however, made a hash of it. He sliced his kick so badly that the ball finished up nearer the centre-circle than the penalty box. It was the first sign of nerves by any England player who'd been in action so far. Mark felt distinctly heartened. He couldn't help it.

'Twang!' remarked Tommy Archbold as he caught up with the kicker. It was an oblique reference to the nickname he himself had invented for his team-mate. Its origin seemed complex to everyone else, but Tommy's explanation was that Billy Hilton reduced to Billy Hilly and when that was reversed it became Hillbilly; and hillbillies all played the guitar, pronounced 'gee-tar' with a hard 'g'.

And so Gee-tar Billy Hilton had henceforth become.

He didn't look his usual easy-going self now, though, as he chased back into midfield to try and help stem the first Dutch attack. Their supporters gave them great encouragement as the ball was whisked out to the left flank.

It was seized on by the player the England manager regarded as the mainspring of the Dutch side: easily identified by his sparrow-like legs and hair cut almost to the scalp, Van Vollenhoven moved in the style of a ballet dancer. Switching the ball from foot to foot and tip-tapping forward with languid ease, he moved in-field. David Redmile back-pedalled, his eyes never leaving the ball. Mark, glancing at his manager, saw that Terry Mercer's lips had tightened into a thin line.

With the sudden change of pace that everyone had been expecting, Van Vollenhoven switched to the left, leaned to the right and, startlingly, next instant was sprinting along the touchline. David, however, had known just what to expect. He could turn as fast as almost any forward, as he now demonstrated, to the astonishment of many of the fans waving Dutch flags. Van Vollenhoven still appeared to be gliding away rather than running. Redmile hardly had need to exert himself before going in with a perfectly judged sliding tackle to sweep the ball into touch. The Dutch boy stumbled, appeared to regain his balance and then fell heavily.

The linesman flagged furiously instead of simply marking the place where the ball had gone out of play. Arms flapping, the referee arrived to have a cautionary word with the England captain and award a free kick against him. David semed to be on the point of protesting and then accepted the rebuke gracefully enough.

'He's done that early in the game to show 'em who's in charge,' announced Doc Manton unnecessarily. 'Continentals don't like tackles from behind. In fact, they hate 'em. Quite legitimate, though, that was – good tackle actually. Stopped the rot.

Terry Mercer said nothing. He didn't need to: at the previous day's training session he'd firmly lectured the squad on the risks of tackling from behind. The penalties for that, he'd pointed out, were usually severe on foreign soil, however skilfully the tackle was made. Mark guessed that the manager was pleased that David Redmile hadn't attempted to argue with the official.

From the kick the ball was hoisted high into the England penalty area. For once Digger misjudged his leap, and Jimmy Kennan, trying to volley the ball to safety, sliced his kick. In the frantic scramble for possession there was a good deal of hacking and cursing until a Dutch attacker managed to get in a snap shot. Unsighted by the press of players around him, Keith Bridgeman didn't even move as the ball struck the underside of the crossbar and bounded back into the penalty area at an acute angle. It reached Van Vollenhoven, standing only fractionally inside the box. Audaciously, he executed a back-heel flick with extraordinary deftness and delicacy. The ball described a perfect parabola and was falling just inside the far post when Keith, diving full-length, got to it. It struck his outstretched hand and, somehow, he managed to steer it round the post and over the line for a corner kick. Practically every other player had been rooted to the spot, hypnotised by the trajectory and Van Vollenhoven's nonchalant effort to score.

Even the crowd took a moment to wake up, and then, like a salute of cannons, firecrackers began to explode again in several parts of the stadium. Holland, second favourites to win the tournament, appeared to have won the support of many of the neutral spectators.

'We'll have to clamp down on that sparrow-legged joker,'

muttered Doc Manton. 'If he keeps that up we'll be in the mire in no time. Could do with a bit of the treatment from Digger, don't you think, Terry?'

The Boss didn't deign to answer, rather to Mark's surprise. After all, he was fairly sure that Mercer wasn't averse to employing intimidatory tactics. As a player himself, he had a reputation for being a hard man, one with a killer instinct when it was needed.

Doc didn't seem to mind not getting a reply. For a few moments longer he moaned quietly to himself about the need to take the pressure off. Mark grinned.

But the pressure wasn't taken off. The Dutch very quickly had gained control of the game and the England defenders were kept at full stretch. Digger, unnerved by something or someone, committed a whole series of mistakes and at one stage David Redmile could be seen remonstrating with him for a scything tackle that led to another free kick for Holland. David himself was playing flawlessly, even though he was finding it increasingly difficult to corral Van Vollenhoven. The Dutch general, however, wasn't trying to beat the opposition by himself; all the time he was varying his tactics and spraying the ball from flank to flank. Then, just when it seemed that he had decided to lay the ball off the instant he received it, he would make a mazy run at the defence, constantly changing his pace to baffle Redmile, his shadow. The Dutch fans were in a ferment of delight at his display.

The England forwards were seeing hardly anything of the ball. Tommy Archbold was angrily patrolling the centre-line like a caged tiger, ready to leap for the freedom of the open spaces of the Dutch half of the field the moment he was given an opening. Mickey Hexton, too, was displaying a good deal of restlessness and regularly dropping back into his own half in the hope of picking up a loose ball. Mark noticed, though, that his room-mate was keeping one eye on the bench in the expectation of being given fresh instructions. They duly came when Mickey dropped back too far in an attempt to give Billy Hilton some assistance.

Imperiously, Terry Mercer waved Mickey forward again, indicating with a stabbing movement of a forefinger that the fair-haired striker should stay up front. Mickey acknowledged the signal and didn't transgress a second time.

The only player who gave the impression that he was perfectly content with the way things were going was Kevin Bonnell. A great believer in conserving energy, he never ran when he could trot or even walk, so inactivity was no hardship for him. He was watching events in the England half with such a detached air that at one point he stood with his arms folded. It was clear to Mark that Terry Mercer had spotted Kevin's stance, but the manager showed no displeasure at such a display of indolence.

The biggest surprise by half-time was that Holland, with the advantage of all their territorial superiority, hadn't taken the lead. Twice they'd come close to doing so but had been thwarted, first by a mis-kick from one of their strikers in front of goal, and then by a breathtaking save from Keith Bridgeman in which he appeared to change direction in mid-air as he fisted a close-range header over the bar.

Terry Mercer stalked off to the dressing-room the moment the whistle blew. Doc raised an eyebrow at Mark but said nothing, as they trailed after him. Doubtless, he was expecting that the Boss would have some cutting comments to make about England's rather desperate performance. Inevitably, Mark was thinking only of which player might be taken off. Trouble was, none of the forwards could be said to have played badly, simply because they'd hardly been in the game yet! If changes were to be made, then it was only logical that they should be in defence.

'Sit up straight!' Mercer snapped in schoolmasterly fashion as soon as everyone had collected something to drink from the refreshment table on the far side of the dressing-room. One or two players were either lolling against the wall or lying at full-stretch on the benches. They obeyed the order without hesitation.

Yet, to the surprise and evident relief of most of them, the manager's remarks turned out to be mild. He had gained their complete attention and that seemed to be his chief aim. It was disappointing, he said, that they hadn't managed to carry the game to their opponents but they'd defended resolutely and shown that they could soak up pressure. That augured well for the way they'd have to cope with the opposition in later matches.

But, he went on, they were giving the midfield away, and if that continued it would prove fatal. He wanted tighter control from the midfield trio of Forster, Wade and Hilton and he wanted to see more long – and accurate – passes out of defence. Up front, England had both pace and power and it must be put to work. With a half-smile he added: 'To paraphrase Winston Churchill, and speaking on behalf of the strikers, it must be a case of "Give us the ball and we'll finish the job" – so, make sure the attackers have something to work with.' One or two players looked baffled by that reference to ancient history but Doc Manton was nodding in vigorous approval.

Lastly, said Mercer, he wanted them to know that he wasn't anxious to make any changes; but he would have to if they were forced on him. After a fractional pause he concluded: 'A settled combination is the aim of every manager. Stay together, play together, win together. Go out and show me you can do it.'

Mark's hopes plummeted. From the outset he'd feared

that he was going to need some luck, or someone else's ill-luck, to get into the game. Yet, as England failed to take any initiative, he began to think that the Boss would have to make a change that would give Mark his chance. Perhaps he would have done if Holland had taken the lead. But, with the score sheet still blank, it was understandable that Mercer should feel that he had still to see the best of the team he'd selected. If only the strikers had made a hash of a few open goals . . .

As the players moved towards the door, Mark joined them. Mickey gave him a smile of sympathy and said softly so that no one else could overhear: 'We could do with you out there, Mark. Your speed would be a great asset.'

That remark was typical of Mickey's generous attitude towards his team-mates. Mark showed his appreciation by slapping him on the shoulder. 'You can do it on your own, Mickey. I hope you get a hat-trick.'

Holland picked up just where they'd left off, running aggressively and pinning England in their own half. Van Vollenhoven began to roam ever wider and was soon operating just as effectively on the right flank. David Redmile appeared to be in a quandary, first sticking rigidly in the Dutch boy's shadow and then tentatively allowing him to go out of range. Mark was baffled. Why on earth hadn't Terry Mercer given his captain explicit instructions to stay with Van Vollenhoven at all costs? Perhaps he had, and David was trying to reconcile his own preference for the right flank with the need to check his tormentor where-ever he went.

The Dutch players were spraying the ball all over the park, first to one wing, then to the other, yet, strangely, were making few really incisive raids into the England goalmouth. Then, against the tide, Jimmy Kennan made a strong run down the centre. Emerging from a melée with the ball, he kept possession, shrugging off a couple of attempted tackles. The Dutch, possibly non-plussed by this unexpected offensive, were slow to assemble their cover. Jimmy competently rounded another opponent and then, with splendid precision, hit a long, diagonal pass to Kevin Bonnell, hovering near the right-hand touchline.

Pouncing on the ball, Kevin killed it with his first touch, swept round his nearest adversary with an ease that astonished the Dutch boy and then cut inside. His air of lassitude had vanished without trace and the orange-shirted opposition were as surprised as their fans by Kevin's determined run. The England striker knew exactly where he was going and what he was going to do when he got there. Several metres from the angle of the box, and while still running strongly, he fired the ball to the far side of the area.

Mickey Hexton, darting away from an opponent, jumped – and, with his left instep raised high, pulled the ball down. Then, as he landed, he stabbed it sideways and into the path of Tommy Archbold.

Typically, Tommy was tearing in with the speed of an express. The ball could not have fallen better for him and his sight of the net was unhampered. All Tommy could think of was bursting it with one of his thunderbolts. From that range it was scarcely credible that he could miss – and Doc Manton was already rising from his seat as Tommy blasted at the ball. But it was his toe that he got under it . . . . and the ball sailed, kite-high, over the bar and the wide running track and into the crowd. And the Dutch fans hooted with derision.

'Oh God, the easiest chance of the match,' moaned the physio, sinking back on to the bench where Mark was squirming with embarrassment for his team-mate.

Tommy was now kicking the turf instead of the ball and even Mickey Hexton could find no word of sympathy for him. The Dutch, of course, could hardly believe their luck, but were eager to make the most of it. From the goal-kick, the ball was cleverly ferried to Van Vollenhoven, who launched himself on another bewildering run; bewildering, that is, only to the England defenders. David Redmile tried to go with him; then, desperately, he threw himself into a crude tackle. The Dutch boy just jinked away from that, the ball still at his feet, and David was left, writhing, on the ground. He made no attempt to get up and it was some moments before the ball went out of play and the referee deigned to inspect the damage to the England captain.

'Get warmed up,' Terry Mercer said curtly to Mark as Doc Manton bustled on to the pitch.

Mark, who had just about given up hope of being called on, stripped off his tracksuit and began sprinting along the running track. He didn't really believe that David would be taken off. He guessed that the full-back had simply taken a slight knock and would quickly recover.

But David was removed to the touchline and Manton remained huddled over him for a long time before signalling across the pitch to the manager. Terry Mercer stood up.

'Right, you're on,' he said to Mark. 'Into the back four. And don't do anything rash.'

'But I'm not a defender!' Mark protested.

'You are now,' Mercer told him unanswerably. Then, as if making a huge concession, he added: 'You can be on the left flank. I'll move Kennan over. He's a two-footed player.'

After a linesman had inspected his studs, Mark was allowed on to the pitch, and while the referee was noting the change, Mercer transmitted fresh instructions to Digger Trowell, now the acting-captain. 'Just keep 'em out – with the big boot if you have to,' was all Digger said to his new defender.

Mark felt distinctly uneasy – and annoyed. The implication of the Boss's remark about Jimmy Kennan was that

Mark was *not* a two-footed player. That might have been true a year or so ago, but since then Mark had been working hard to develop skills with his right foot that matched those of his left. He felt he'd just about succeeded. But there was really no time to think about that now: already the game was beginning to flow around him. Naturally enough, the Holland manager knew that Mark Fox was a striker; therefore the England substitute would be a weakness in the defence – a weakness that had to be exploited to give Holland the advantage they'd been seeking. So Van Vollenhoven drifted over to carve out the openings.

Before he could make any real indentation, however, the England forwards combined effectively for Mickey Hexton to demonstrate that he had as much talent as his opposite number. Put through by an astute flick from Kevin, he bluffed his way past two defenders, and then, as the goalie dashed out to try and smother the ball, Mickey scooped it over him. But the ball struck the base of a post and was scrambled clear.

Mark bit his lip. It was infuriating that he hadn't been up there to round off the movement. He was certain he'd have scored from that position. Although he admired Mickey's skills he felt that he himself was the better finisher. All he wanted was the chance to prove it, to show Terry Mercer how wrong he'd been to leave him out of the forward line. Yet he daren't risk a solo run if he won the ball: he'd been ordered to stay back and he knew he'd be jeopardising his future if he disobeyed.

Only moments later he was wishing he'd never come on to the pitch at all. The Dutch, confident now that England weren't going to get a goal, pushed forward in increased numbers. One of their midfielders stormed down the centre, swung left and then sent a beautiful reverse pass to Van Vollenhoven out on the right. Mark didn't hesitate. He had to make a positive contribution to the game. He charged forward to dispossess the Dutchman.

Exactly as he had done so many times before in the match, Van Vollenhoven brought off a double feint and shuffle to evade a tackle and continued his progress. Mark, fooled, felt furious. He spun round and chased after his opponent. Van Vollenhoven, exchanging a quick one–two with a team-mate, accelerated into the penalty area, intent this time on putting the ball in the net himself. He wasn't aware just how fast Mark Fox could run.

Keith Bridgeman, positive as always when danger threatened, came off his line to dive on the ball at the attacker's feet. The Dutch boy slowed fractionally, ready to take the ball round the goalie, when Mark came in behind him with a sliding tackle. Keith was opening his mouth to yell, 'No, it's mine!' when Mark made contact with the ball, jabbing it away from Van Vollenhoven's feet. Mark had achieved his objective – but in doing so he had also pushed the ball well wide of the advancing goalkeeper. And, with no one else on hand to stop it, the ball rolled over the line and into the net.

As Mark picked himself up, still staring at the ball as it nestled in the back of the net, Keith, hands on knees shouted at him: 'Couldn't you see it was my ball? I had it sewn up. You've given 'em the game, you crazy idiot!' Digger and the other defenders just looked aghast; none of them said a word to Mark. By now, Van Vollenhoven and his cohorts had cavorted back to the centre to the unrestrained joy of their fans.

The one place Mark daren't look was towards the bench: he could imagine only too vividly the expressions on the faces of Mercer and Manton. He felt sick, sick to the pit of his stomach. He'd craved a goal in Europe: and now he'd scored one – for Holland. Unbelievable – unbelievable except for the fact that the referee was about to start the game again because Holland had scored. Correction: a goal had been scored for Holland. By Mark Fox. He'd heard of people saying that they wished the ground would open up and swallow them, and now he knew exactly how they felt. It might have been easier if he'd been playing as a striker, because at least he'd have the chance of cancelling out his error by grabbing the equaliser at the other end.

As it was, he was soon in action again as a defender. Determined to clinch victory with another goal, the Dutch roared back into the attack, and some slipshod work in midfield by Ian Wade allowed their central strikers to cut through easily. Digger brought off one of his crunching tackles and then pushed the ball sideways to Mark, who was thankful to boot it far upfield in the general direction of the England attackers. But he was near enough to the bench to see Terry Mercer give a doleful shake of his head. Mark felt that nothing he did was ever going to please his manager.

Barely three minutes of the match remained when Holland, confident now of the outcome, pushed a couple of their midfielders into the attack and set up another assault. Again it was Digger who broke it up with a fine, ball-winning tackle; he pushed a pass to Billy Hilton who then nudged the ball to Mark.

Even as he seized on the pass, Mark knew exactly what he was going to do. Not a gram of his energy had yet been sapped: and an explosive burst of speed was one of his greatest assets. Head down, he powered out of his own half of the pitch, leaving two opponents stranded by sheer pace as he rounded them. Tommy Archbold, already on the move, hared down the middle with Mickey Hexton running a parallel course on the left flank. Kevin was signalling for the ball but Mark ignored him. Taking a diagonal course, he swept past another orange-shirt, changed direction again and then, from outside the box, unleashed a tremendous shot.

His aim was for the far bottom corner of the net and, as he'd hoped, the ball curved late. The goalie could see it all the way as he dived but the pace of the shot and its swing almost beat him. But he reached it and diverted it across the bye-line for a corner. Mark had no time to experience despair. Kevin raced to take the kick, the penalty area suddenly was as crowded as a tube station in rush-hour, opponents jostling each other for position, and everyone seemed aware that the last seconds of the match were ticking away.

The cross was well-flighted, but too far from the goal-line. A defender headed it out powerfully, straight to Mark, standing just outside the box for just such a chance. With his left foot, and on the volley, he hit it back with all the force he possessed. Inevitably, it struck someone on the body, ricocheted across the area, bobbed up as another player tried to control it – and then, with complete fear-lessness, Mickey Hexton flung himself forward into the midst of boots and knees and ankles. With the top of his head he made contact with the ball and sent it spinning into the net, only millimetres above the turf.

For a moment or two Mickey seemed as stunned as the Holland team. Then, in disbelief, he kept repeating: 'I've scored, I've scored for England!' He hardly appeared to notice when Mark congratulated him. Terry Mercer had actually got to his feet, though he still hadn't crossed the running track.

No one, Mark realised, had congratulated him, in spite of the fact that he'd set up the goal. Without his run, and the subsequent corner kick, England wouldn't have equal-ised. He could only hope that the Boss appreciated his contribution.

But, when the final whistle blew and the players went off with the score 1–1, Mercer said not a word to him.

Chapter Seven

DISASTER AT THUN

Tommy Archbold had been counting for most of the journey. 'Hey,' he said excitedly, still peering through the coach window. 'Do you know what? That's the sixth shooting gallery I've seen. They must be mad keen on guns in this country.'

'Not shooting galleries, you Scouse nit,' laughed Kevin Bonnell. 'Rifle ranges! Target practice – for real rifles. For marksmen.'

'Same thing,' said Tommy imperturbably. 'They're for shooting. I fancy that. I fancy a spell in the Army with the professionals, roaring around in tanks and blasting off some of those armour-piercing weapons. Great, that.'

'If you couldn't shoot straighter than you did against Holland they'd have you out in no time," Digger told him.

'Watch it, wack!' Tommy retaliated with mock threats. 'I could shoot a hole through you any day, any distance. I wouldn't need armour-piercing bullets, either.'

'But what do the Swiss need all those rifle ranges for?' asked Billy Hilton. 'I mean, they've always been neutral in wars, haven't they? So they don't have soldiers or armies.'

'Yes, they do,' said Kevin promptly. It was becoming clear to all of them that his knowledge of the country at least matched Mickey Hexton's. His casual attitude on the football field obviously bore no relation to his attention in

87

the classroom. 'The Swiss have quite a big army because every man has to serve in it at some time. They all have to put in time on the rifle ranges and they all have their own rifles that they look after themselves. They want to make sure they're not going to get clobbered if anybody does start a war.'

'Well, they're not much good at shooting into the net,' remarked Tommy, determined to stay in the conversation. He was referring to the previous day's match, when Switzerland had been defeated 0–3 by West Germany. The score could have been higher, but the general opinion was that the favourites had taken it easy against the host nation. After their disappointment over the Holland match, the result of the second match of the tournament had heartened the England squad. Their next match was against Switzerland, and they felt they could win it convincingly. Then, if, as expected, West Germany beat Holland, they and England would be the top two teams in the competition. Terry Mercer had made it plain that he expected nothing less.

The coach trip had been laid on by the tournament organisers to give the boys a break from training and playing, and to allow them to see more of the scenic splendours of Switzerland. Although it was believed that the various national squads would be going to different destinations, Mr Mercer, who made a point of inquiring into everything, had learned that it was perfectly possible that the coach parties would meet somewhere or other. So he had instructed his players that, if they did happen to run into them, they were 'not to fraternise with the opposition'.

'As I've told you all before,' the Boss had stated, 'we've come here to win. You can enjoy yourselves perfectly well without being in the company of our opponents. At home you won't find the players of, say, Manchester United and

Liverpool going off to a funfair together the day before they're due to meet in a Cup-tie. They keep their distance because they need to keep a keen, cutting edge when so much is at stake. If you get too pally with an opponent, that cutting edge can very easily be blunted, and therefore useless when the knives are out.'

'You know,' said Billy Hilton when the Boss had departed, 'when they knew I was coming to Switzerland, somebody told me it was supposed to be the playground of the world. The way Mercer talks, you'd think it was a battleground for the World Cup.'

Now, as the motor coach negotiated a sharp turn in the town of Thun, none of the players was in the mood to think about warfare on or off the football pitch. It had been a longer journey, part of it by train, than they'd expected, and all they were concerned about was getting out of the bus and enjoying themselves. The town itself was an obvious attraction: Ian Wade, who was always interested in history, pointed out the castle with its four towers, and said that it made the whole place look like something out of the middle ages. He must have been reading it up because he knew that in another castle on the lake side there was a war museum. With a grin, he invited Tommy Archbold to explore it with him. Scornfully, Tommy replied that he wanted something a bit more up-to-date: predictably, he was going off in search of a shooting gallery. Others had already decided that they were going to look round the shops – some in fascinating-looking arcades off the main street – to buy souvenirs and presents. But, on a sultry day, the lake – Thunersee – had the greatest appeal for the majority.

Mark, who had no clear ideas of what he really wanted to do, wasn't at all surprised to find that he was going to have Mickey Hexton as a companion. 'What shall we do?' the blond boy asked eagerly, as Mark and Keith

Bridgeman hovered, undecided, outside a wooden café decked out in cheerful colours, with tables on its long, railed verandah.

'Oh, I fancy a sail on the lake,' said Keith, who was never inclined to exert himself at anything. 'I reckon I could get some decent pictures of the mountains out there – especially the Jungfrau.'

'Well, we could hire a boat, I expect,' said Mickey. 'I mean, I don't mind doing the rowing – well, some of it!'

'Not likely!' Keith said sharply. 'That's too much like hard work. What we want is just a lazy cruise on one of those big boats. Stretch ourselves out on the top deck. Peaceful. Bit of luxury. That's the life, eh, Mark?'

'Oh, sure. Suits me. Whatever you like.'

By now, the rest of the squad, scattering in twos and threes, had vanished, and Mickey, pleased to act as pathfinder, led his room-mates down to the landing stage. They could see one of the white boats, proudly flying the Swiss flag at the stern, out on the lake, and it appeared to be heading in their direction. Mark was still feeling subdued, and the heaviness of the atmosphere wasn't helping to lift his mood. It had occurred to him that by now he ought to have at least sent off some postcards, but he couldn't be bothered. Anyway, his parents would know he was safe: had anything gone wrong with the trip they'd have read reports about it in the paper. His mind was preoccupied with the next match and his chances of being picked to play.

Mickey, bubbling with enthusiasm for every new experience, darted away to buy ice-cream for the three of them. They lounged on a wooden seat to eat it while watching the steamer's approach. Mickey was chattering away about nothing in particular when, suddenly, he stopped in mid-sentence.

Aware of the tension, Keith turned to look at him and asked: 'What's up, then?'

'That man over there, by the cabin-thing,' Mickey said softly. 'The one in the pale blue jacket and peaked-cap. He's the one who was looking at me, staring at me, at Zurich Airport. I *know* he is. And he's still staring at me.'

Keith glanced casually in that direction. 'Probably just wants your autograph because he knows you're going to be a famous international in a few years,' he said lightly. 'You'll just have to get used to living with instant fame, Mick.'

'I can guess what he really wants,' Mickey said, quite fiercely now. 'He wants me. I know all about men who want to interfere with young boys. The Warden's always going on about them. They have a funny look in their eyes.'

'He looks quite normal to me,' said Mark, who'd been studying the man. 'Anyway, he's just reading his paper. He's not interested in you, Mickey.'

'But he is, Mark, I can tell,' Mickey insisted. 'It was just the same at the airport: I could feel his eyes boring right into me. He's got a-a-fixation. I just don't want him near me.'

'Look, mate, calm down, will you?' Keith told him gently. 'We're all together, there are three of us. Nothing can happen if we stick together. And we'll be in a crowd on that boat. Looks pretty full to me from here. Anyway, we don't even know if he's going to get on the boat – he may just be meeting someone.'

Mickey was unconvinced. 'He must have known we were coming to Thun; it'd be easy enough for anyone to find out where the teams were going for their day out. So he's followed us – me. Must have. I tell you, it's just me he's interested in. I could tell that at the airport.'

'So what do you want us to do?' Mark asked.

'Oh, let's get away from here, Mark, please! I'd feel – trapped – if he came on the boat after us. I know you'll think it's crazy but I just don't want him anywhere near us.'

By now the lake steamer was turning to come into the landing stage. People who'd been waiting began to edge forward. The man in the blue jacket was folding his paper. Even Mark had the impression that the fellow was deliberately not looking in their direction.

Decisively, he stood up. 'O.K., then, let's push off on our own. Hey, we *could* hire our own boat after all and still go out on the lake. I don't mind doing a bit of the rowing.'

Keith was starting to let out a mock-groan of dismay, but, catching sight of Mickey's expression, he quickly cut off the sound. 'Fair enough,' he substituted hurriedly. 'Like I said, anything for a bit of peace.'

Mark was feeling much better. The thought of being involved in some action was very appealing, even if it was only rowing a small boat. Glancing back, however, as they left the landing stage, he noted that Blue Jacket was no longer disguising his interest in them. Avidly was how he was watching them – yet he appeared to be making no move to follow them.

'Come on, let's move,' Mark said, breaking into a jog. Keith shot him looks of silent protest but he, too, increased the pace.

'Look, I think we can hire a boat over there – that bloke seems to have a fleet of them,' Mickey said, indicating a small jetty lined with craft. 'And it's *my* treat – I haven't spent anything yet so I've plenty of money.'

Mark was about to protest when Mickey cut him off. 'No, Mark, you're both doing this for my sake. I *want* to pay.'

So they let him go ahead and negotiate a price with the

boatman, a stocky figure with rimless spectacles and rope-soled canvas shoes.

It was some moments before Mickey, after fumbling awkwardly to get at his money, clinched a deal. The boatman more than once jerked an expressive thumb at the sky and when Mickey ushered them into a rowing boat, smartly painted in red-and-white, Keith inquired what the fellow had been going on about.

'Well, of course, he was talking in another language so I didn't quite get the hang of it – but he did say "mauvais temps" a few times. That's bad weather, isn't it?'

'Yeah,' said Keith casting a disbelieving eye at the sky. 'Must be one of his jokes. The Swiss are great jokers, you know.'

'Oh, are they?' said Mickey innocently. 'I hadn't realised it. They all seem a bit, well, *depressed*, to me.'

'It's all these mountains,' said Keith airily. 'Makes 'em feel a bit shut in. Now, Mick, let's head that way, towards the Jungfrau. That's the one, with all the snow on it and the double peak.'

He lay back in the stern and fiddled knowingly with the lens of his camera, newly-acquired for the trip. More than once he'd told Mark that he fancied the idea of becoming a professional photographer when his playing career was over. He was confident that people would be queuing up to have their portraits taken by a former England goalkeeper and he would get commissions to photograph famous sights all over the world.

Mark, whose offer to take the oars for the first stretch had been indignantly rejected by Mickey, contentedly gazed at the receding shore. The passenger boat was already well out into the lake and he wondered whether Blue Jacket was on board. He still found it hard to believe that the man really was so interested in Mickey. More likely he was a football fan who'd remembered seeing them at the airport and knew that their next match was against his own country, Switzerland. Satisfied with that explanation he closed his eyes and listened to the distant tinklings of cow bells as the herds grazed on the slopes.

'The light seems to be getting worse,' Keith announced after a lengthy period of silence, broken only by the slap of the oars and the sounds of Mickey's exertions. 'Can't you get this ocean liner to go a bit faster, Mick? If I shoot from this distance those mountains will look like pimples.'

'It's hard work, rowing,' Mickey panted. 'I'm doing my best, Keith – but it's so, so hot. I think the heat's draining my energy away.'

'I warned you, I warned you,' the goalkeeper reminded him cheerfully. 'It was you that wanted to be the galley slave – so slave on, lad, slave on!'

Mark sat up. 'I'll take over, Mickey. Time you had a rest. Your shirt's absolutely soaked in sweat. Why don't you take it off?'

'No, I'm O.K., Mark, thanks. But I wouldn't mind a break. We seem to have been out here for ages.'

'I know, you must have rowed several nautical miles already,' said Mark, balancing precariously as he took Mickey's place. He had already stripped off his own shirt but, even though the sun had now vanished, it seemed to be getting still warmer. Trouble was, there wasn't so much as a breath of wind to cool things down. Steadfastly, he kept the boat moving silkily along Keith's chosen course, though it was hardly without effort. As Mickey said, rowing quickly sapped your energy.

The first crack of thunder was so startlingly loud that all three of them looked around for signs of an explosion. The sound echoed across the lake as if it had been bounced back from the wall of mountains. Mark, very nearly catching a crab, was recovering his stroke as lightning stabbed vividly. Then, against a sky that quickly had turned the colour of charred wood, the flashes followed each other so rapidly that the effect was like a firework display.

'Hey, that's really something!' Keith yelled admiringly above the rolling cannon-fire of thunder. 'Might get a fantastic picture – fantastic!'

Involuntarily, Mark shivered. The heat had gone, swept away instantly, it seemed, by a current of chilling air. With an ease that surprised him, he swung the boat round and pulled for the shore.

'Hey,' Keith shouted again, this time in protest. 'Where're you going? I was just lining up the best shot yet. I've never seen so much lightning. I could win a prize with any of these pictures.'

'*If* they ever come out – *if* we ever get back,' Mark muttered to himself. He had an idea the worst was yet to come. What he couldn't work out was whether they'd be safer in the middle of the lake or back on dry land. He called over his shoulder: 'Are you O.K., Mickey?'

'Oh, yes!' was the excited reply. 'I agree with Keith, it's just fantastic. I've never seen anything like it. I never thought I would. I read about the storms they have sometimes in Switzerland. All the force sort of gets concentrated on one small area because of the mountains, like in a big bowl, you know.'

'Oh, yeah,' said Mark non-committally. He'd decided they'd be better off back on shore. He was sweating quite freely now for the temperature seemed to have risen again. He thought it was about time Keith offered to do his share of rowing.

The rain smashed down on them. Arriving without warning, the force and coldness of it on his bare shoulders made Mark gasp aloud. It fell like a waterfall, a continuous cascade, hammering into the surface of the lake so that it appeared to the three boys in the boat that they were encircled by fountains.

Desperately, Keith tried to shield his camera. But, like his companions, he was wearing only a thin shirt and already it was sodden. Mark saw with astonishment that the rain was virtually obscuring Keith's features as it streamed down his face.

It was becoming almost impossible to row: the deluge was battering at Mark's arms and legs and in spite of his grip on the oars he found he couldn't force them to work. No longer could he see where they were heading, if they were moving at all, and he could see nothing beyond the stern of the boat except the rain. All he was conscious of was the water, the turbulent and now terrifying water. Even his feet had disappeared.

'The boat's filling up!' he roared above the din. 'She's filling up! We're sinking!'

Chapter Eight

OPERATION RED CROSS

Keith didn't appear to comprehend the situation. He was still trying to protect his camera – an impossible task – holding it tight against his chest under his shirt. He kept trying to peer at the sky as though for signs that the rain would stop.

The level of the water was rising visibly. It was now well above Mark's ankles. He felt a hand on his shoulder and, twisting round, glimpsed the whiteness of Mickey's face through the curtain of rain. Even in such desperate circumstances it registered with him that Mickey's manner was remarkably calm.

'We've got to bail out, Mark,' the younger boy was telling him. 'It's our only chance.'

Mark misunderstood completely. 'Get out of the boat, you mean? That's crazy. We couldn't swim from –'

'No, no! I mean, bail the *water* out. Scoop it out with something, anything.'

But what? Mark cast around for something that would answer their need, but there was nothing that was of any use. They had been carrying nothing when they hired the boat. It was Mickey himself who thought of something.

'Our shoes! We've got to use them – all of us.'

Keith still wasn't heeding their plight. Mark, fumblingly removing one of his own shoes while retaining a grip on the oars, jabbed at his team-mate with his foot.

'Get bailing!' he ordered. Keith just looked bewildered. 'I've got to save the camera,' he muttered pleadingly.

'We've got to save our *lives*,' Mark yelled. 'To hell with your camera!'

Keith had the look of someone about to start an argument, but, having taken further measures to secure his camera round his neck, he wrenched off a shoe and began bailing with that. Mickey was hard at work, slopping water over the side as fast as he could. Mark had to abandon thoughts of helping them: it was difficult enough to retain his grasp of the oars without trying to act as a third bailer.

Thunder was still booming, though less deafeningly and at longer intervals. But visibility hadn't improved and the struggle to drag the boat through the water was no easier, in spite of the efforts of Mickey and Keith to lower the level of the rainwater. It seemed to Mark that, if anything, it was getting higher. The ache in his arms had become a pain, a pain that was intensifying. He had to have a rest. His head sank, his shoulders drooped.

D

'You've got to keep going, Mark!' Mickey yelled at him. 'If we start drifting we'll have had it. There are currents in this lake and they could carry us anywhere.'

Mark knew that, but his muscles just wouldn't respond. He pulled on the oars as hard as he could and made no headway whatsoever.

'I'll take over again,' Mickey volunteered. 'You need a rest. Just shift over a bit.'

'No!' Mark shouted. Already the slight rocking motion caused by Mickey's movements threatened further danger. 'Stay where you are. I can – '

The wave which suddenly slapped up against the port side of the rowing boat could only have been caused by a large vessel. It struck at precisely the moment that Mickey was attempting to step over the seat.

Mark, feeling the boat keeling over, was trying to right it when Keith screamed at him: 'Mickey's gone overboard! He's fallen in!'

There had been no cry from Mickey himself, no splash as he landed in the water: or, if there had been the sounds had been drowned by the battering rain. The boat bobbed on the passing waves and Mark, with renewed determination tried to bring her round by using a single oar.

'Over there, over there,' Keith was directing. 'Can he swim?'

Gasping for air and shaking his head fiercely to clear water from his eyes, Mickey appeared to be on the point of going under again. Then, to his companions' vast relief, he suddenly struck out towards the boat. For someone of so slight a physique, Mickey was obviously a quite powerful swimmer. He came up to the side of the boat in very few strokes. He was reaching for the rowlock, and Keith was leaning out to help him, when Mark, realising what could happen, yelled a warning.

'No, Mickey, not there! You'll turn us right over. Grab hold of the stern.'

Luckily for all of them, Mickey understood the danger. Nodding his head, he manœuvred himself round the boat. He even managed to give the impression that he was perfectly content to be where he was. His calmness astonished Mark. Yet Mickey was bound to have suffered a severe shock.

'Are you all right, Mick? I mean, you're not hurt are you?' Keith wanted to know.

'Not – not too bad. The – the water – the water's terribly cold.'

Keith looked across at Mark. 'We've got to get him back in the boat. He just can't stay out there.'

Mark knew that. But he was afraid of what might happen when they attempted to drag Mickey in. It now seemed to him to be the most fragile boat he'd ever known. One wrong move and it would turn turtle: he was certain of that, too.

Then, just as suddenly as it had come, the rain died away. It was as if a curtain had been lifted. The sight of the mountains, the distant green slopes, the deep red roofs of buildings, the activity on the lake itself, astonished Mark. The storm had lasted less than half an hour and yet it seemed to him that the three of them had been in a world of their own, entirely cut off from everyone and everything else, for half a lifetime.

'Thank heavens for that,' breathed Keith, looking up at a sky that was already clearing. Then, glancing back at Mickey he said: 'Come on, Mick, we'll get you in. Just have to do it very carefully.'

Mark was still apprehensive about the operation. Though the boat contained a lot of water, that wasn't helping to stabilise it: the reverse, if anything. He was fearful that any tilting at all would plunge them all into the lake. Could he manage to row them back to the shore with Mickey clinging to the stern? No, impossible. Mickey couldn't survive a trip like that.

He was so preoccupied with the problem, that the cabin cruiser heading directly towards them was almost on them before Mark became aware of its existence. For a terrible moment he thought it was going to run them down. But they'd been spotted all right. There was a change in the surging note of the engines, the vessel sheered away to one side of them and then slowed almost to a stop.

'Oh, great!' exclaimed Keith. 'We're going to be rescued.'

Someone was hailing from the deck but they couldn't make out the words. The language, Mark recognised, was German.

'We're English – ENGLISH. Need help – HELP.' Keith wasted not a moment in getting the message across.

'O.K., O.K., we help,' was the immediate reply from a man standing behind the cockpit and using a loud-hailer. 'Remain calm! We come alongside.'

His English was obviously excellent, his accent nearly faultless. Mark experienced a great sense of relief. The cruiser was beautifully sleek, painted in dark and light blue and flying the Swiss flag at the stern. Mark tried to help by steering the rowing boat towards her.

'O.K., O.K., you sit still – we get you both off. We have steps. Lowering them now.' The cruiser's skipper, if that's what he was, had taken charge. The steps turned out to be a ship's ladder, short, but invaluable in the circumstances.

'Our–friend–is–in–the–water,' Keith was yelling up at their rescuer. 'He–fell–in. Can–you–get–him–out–first?'

Until that moment, the man hadn't noticed that there was a third boy clinging to the rowing boat . . . He immediately issued some instructions in his own language to whoever was in the cabin and, two girls suddenly appeared on deck. Displaying great agility, the skipper slithered down the ladder and, as the two vessels came together, he leaned down and effortlessly swept Mickey up and out of the water. In moments he had been lifted on to the deck and one of the girls was wrapping a huge towel round him.

Keith followed, scorning offers of assistance and climbing unaided, and then the skipper took Mark's place in the rowing boat.

'You go up,' he said firmly but with a grin. 'I look after your ship. No trouble. It will be O.K. You go and get clean.'

Mark supposing that 'dry' was what was meant, didn't linger. He was thankful to get out of the boat and hoped that he might never see it again

When he reached the deck, one of the girls stepped forward to offer him a voluminous towel. She was very pretty, with reddish-blonde hair and smiling brown eyes, and he thought she probably wasn't all that much older than himself. Beckoning him, she led the way down into the cabin, which surprised him by its spaciousness. It all looked very luxurious.

Keith, towelling himself vigorously, grinned a greeting: 'Hey, great this, isn't it? Told you I fancied a real cruise.'

'Yeah, I can see why now,' replied Mark as the other girl entered the cabin. She, too, was fair-haired but appeared rather less friendly. Nonetheless, it was apparent that she wanted to help. Kneeling, she opened a locker beneath one of the bunks that doubled as a bench seat and was strewn with cushions, and took out several sweaters and pairs of slacks.

'Dry clothes,' she said in a hard, clipped accent. 'For you, please.'

Then, after exchanging glances, the two girls discreetly left the cabin.

Keith quickly sorted through the clothing and for himself picked a grey sweater and dark brown trousers which fitted tolerably well. Mark caught a wry glance from Mickey and could guess what the boy was thinking: that he seemed to be spending much of his time in Switzerland removing his clothes, or having them removed for him. The slacks that were left for him were much too big but, as he remarked, he was just thankful for anything that would help him to feel warm again.

After admiring the contents of the cabin, which had pictures hung on the walls, Keith stated the obvious: 'Must be worth a fortune. I reckon we've been picked up by millionaires!'

That view appeared to be confirmed when the remaining member of the crew came in holding a bottle of cognac and a tray of glasses.

'You have a drink, yes? To make you feel good again, I think.'

'Just what we need, mate,' said Keith enthusiastically as the man poured generous measures for all of them. Mark thought he was probably in his early twenties, and so perhaps a few years younger than the skipper. They were dressed identically, however, in light blue, short-sleeved cotton shirts and dark blue slacks, the colours in which their boat was painted.

Mickey looked askance at the brandy but Mark insisted that he drank it all down. 'I'll help you get over the shock of being in the water. It's good for you.'

Grimacing, Mickey obeyed.

'Ah, good, I see that my brother has been looking after you correctly,' said the skipper as he entered the cabin, followed by the girls. 'Now, I think we should introduce ourselves. This is my brother Gunther, that is his friend, Paula, this is my friend, Bruni, and my name is Marc.'

There was a formal shaking of hands all round and

102

Marc seemed highly delighted that he had a namesake among his guests, even though it was quickly established that the spellings were different.

'I have dealt with the problem of your little boat,' Marc said, without specifying exactly what he had done. 'It has come to no harm. Nor have you, I think. You all look much healthier. I think you have a liking for brandy, yes?'

Keith said, yes, he was certainly developing a taste for it and, as if on cue, Gunther gave him some more. Paula, the red-haired girl, murmured something to Gunther in German, who nodded and then asked the boys if they were hungry.

'Yeah, absolutely famished,' replied Keith, who plainly saw himself as the spokesman for the survivors.

'Good, good. Then we will have food in a few minutes,' said Marc. 'The girls will be happy to prepare it for you. I regret, their English is not very good. They can understand it but not speak it well. It is so with my brother. I am sorry.'

'Oh, that's all right,' said Keith airily. Mickey laughed, but Mark felt somewhat embarrassed: after all, he himself could understand barely a word of German and his French was little better. Keith asked: 'Who's driving your boat at the moment? I mean, Gunther was steering when we came aboard.'

'Oh, do not worry, Keith,' Marc smiled. 'The ship is on auto-control at this time, so we are not in danger! Now, please, tell me about yourselves. You are in Switzerland on holiday, yes?'

Inevitably, it was Keith who launched into an explanation of their visit, and, as soon as he learned that they were footballers, Marc was so delighted that he summoned his brother from the after-cabin. Both of them knew a good deal about the tournament, for, it turned out, they were not only keen supporters of F.C. Zurich but watched their national team whenever they could. Marc questioned them closely about the Holland team, Switzerland's next opponents after playing England.

Naturally, Keith had already told them that he was the goalkeeper and Marc, being an excellent host, turned to Mark to ask him where he played.

'Well, er, actually, I'm not – ' Mark started to say.

'He's a striker and he's brilliant,' Mickey cut in, to Mark's relief. He hadn't relished trying to explain that he was merely a substitute; his candour wouldn't allow him to admit anything else.

'And you, Mickey, do you play as well? I think perhaps you are one of the reserves, yes?'

'Oh, no, he's a striker, too – and he creates the chances for the rest of us,' Mark put in quickly, balancing the books. 'He's an absolutely vital member of the side.'

Mickey gave him a shy smile of gratitude as Marc glanced from one to the other. But before anything more could be said, Bruni came forward to say that they should eat now. They filed into the after-cabin where a table had been set up. Keith's eyes glittered when he saw that there were plates of cold meat, bowls of different kinds of salad, two loaves still to be cut and an abundance of fresh fruit.

'You will drink some wine, yes?' asked Marc, uncorking a bottle of hock.

'Oh, sure, great!' replied Keith, and they all laughed.

Mark had never known his friend in such sparkling form, and, over the meal, it was the goalkeeper, who, by direct questioning, elicited some information about their hosts. The brothers shared a house in Zurich, where all four of them lived, and while Marc worked for a bank (though he didn't disclose in what capacity) Gunther was a chemist.

'You mean you have a shop?' asked Mickey innocently.

The girls appeared to understand that well enough for both of them burst out laughing.

'No, no, my friend,' Marc grinned. 'He does not sell toothpaste! He works for a big firm that makes drugs. It is of international importance.'

Soon, however, the talk turned back to football, to the despair of Paula who threw her hands up in mock surrender as soon as the subject was mentioned. 'Mein Gott! Mein Gott!' she murmed. They discussed the strengths of various teams and Marc, shaking his head sadly, confessed that Switzerland were not yet of world class at any level.

'You will defeat us easily when you play us the day after tomorrow,' he forecast.

'Will you be going to the match?' asked Mark. He was wondering if it would be possible for Terry Mercer to get special seats for them as a way of saying thank you for the rescue.

'Ah, I would like to do that but, unhappily, it will not be possible,' replied Marc, looking genuinely regretful. 'I must be working then – it is not a time for watching football. Time, my young friend, is money, especially for a banker!'

None of the boys had really been conscious of the passage of time since setting out on the lake. When they learned how late it was Mark grew alarmed, for in half an hour they were due to report back to the coach for the return to Zurich. When he raised the matter rather tentatively with their host, however, Marc insisted that they should all travel back to Zurich together in his car.

'We rescued you, so you are our responsibility until we know you are safe and well at home – in your case, at your training camp,' he said suavely. 'You are our guests now, you see, and it is the Swiss tradition to look after guests correctly. Did you know, this is the country where the Red Cross organization was started, now almost a hundred years ago? The founder, he, too, was a banker! So I must honour his memory.'

'Er, thanks, Marc, thanks very much,' said Mark. 'But you see, we have to get back to the bus because it'll be waiting for us. And if we're very late . . .'

'That is not a problem. This ship is equipped with radio-telephone. So I shall telephone a friend in Thun and he will inform your driver that you will be travelling to Zurich by car. That will be satisfactory for everyone, yes?'

'Great,' exclaimed Keith with a Cheshire cat smile. 'Then we can get some sunbathing in on the rest of the voyage – and I'll get those close-ups of the mountains. All right if we go up on deck now, Marc?'

Mark's raised eyebrows were ignored by his team-mates. But he couldn't help worrying about Terry Mercer's possible reaction to their unorthodox, and unauthorised, trip.

If there were trouble, Mark was positive he would be the one to suffer most. For some reason he still didn't understand, he was completely out of favour with the Boss, who needed no excuse at all to keep him out of the team. It was all right for Keith because he was a vital part of the squad and so had little to fear in the matter of reprisals; while Mickey, too, would undoubtedly remain *in* favour for several reasons.

All the same, Mark managed to enjoy the rest of the day. Keith, affected no doubt by the cognac and the wine, was in very high spirits and had everyone laughing at his antics when he decided to demonstrate how he kept goal (once he very nearly dived over the rails into the lake). Although they plainly couldn't understand much of what Keith was saying, the girls got a lot of fun out of it, too, Mark was captivated by Paula's habit of exclaiming 'Mein Gott!' at frequent intervals and wrinkling her nose at the

106

same time. He wished there were a chance of her becoming his girl friend one day; it seemed to him that neither Gunther nor Marc displayed much affection for, or even interest in, the girls.

After disembarking from the cabin cruiser at a private mooring, they climbed into a large white Mercedes: Mickey was squeezed in between the girls, who had made rather a fuss of him, and, just as predictably, Keith was in the front with the two men. Mark was perfectly content to be sitting beside Paula. Driving with dashing style and often enough using only one hand to cope with vicious turns and gradients, Marc kept up a constant chatter about football, Switzerland, money and what he described as 'England's very great fortune' in being surrounded by water. He had a yearning to do some ocean sailing and much regretted the fact that his own country was land-locked.

Then, after an uncharacteristic pause he announced: 'It has been a good day, a very good day. We have become excellent friends. So, we should celebrate our friendship correctly, with a good dinner. You will be my guests, and I will drive you to your training camp.'

Protests were quite useless, as even Mickey discovered (naturally, Keith didn't make any). Pulling up at the next telephone kiosk, he contacted the college and explained that three of the England players would be returning a little later than expected; beamingly, he told his excellent friends, as he slid behind the wheel again, that all was well. They accepted it. By now they were well aware that Marc was a superb organiser. Following another radio-telephone call from the cabin cruiser, even their rowing boat had been taken care of by another associate of his when they landed. Doubtless, it had already been returned to its owner.

Rather to Mark's surprise, the house where the brothers lived was not a chalet on the edge of a meadow with spectacular views, but a tall, slender building in a business street in the heart of the city. It was appointed as sumptuously as the cabin cruiser. The fillet steaks they were served were superb but, by unspoken agreement, the boys were decidedly cautious about how much wine they drank, and this time they declined the cognac.

'You feed well, you play well – but not too well, perhaps,' chortled Marc several times. 'We do not want to be defeated too badly when you play us.'

They were thankful they were not playing Switzerland the next day as Marc drove them to the college. When they parted from him it was with mutual vows of continuing friendship.

Terry Mercer was waiting for them just inside the entrance. The hall was dimly lit but Mark could detect the expression on the Boss's face.

Mark drew in his breath sharply. 'Mein Gott!' he muttered to himself.

Chapter Nine

GOAL IN EUROPE

It was, and they all knew it, their last chance. None of the squad needed reminding of that. Unless they defeated West Germany they would be, barring a miracle, out of the tournament. They would return home without having recorded a single victory in the competition.

With the rest of the England players, Mark was listening as attentively as possible to Terry Mercer giving what seemed like his umpteenth pep talk. The team for this vital match had yet to be announced, so Mark still had no idea whether he would be playing. On balance, he thought it unlikely. On the other hand, because an outright win was essential, the Boss would have to play to his attacking strength – and that meant including his main strikers.

If England beat West Germany, then they would definitely gain a place in the final, the play-off match between the teams which finished in the first two places in the League table. Even if England drew, they still had a chance, albeit a remote one, of contesting the final. But for that to happen, Switzerland would have to overcome Holland in their last game: and such a result hardly seemed likely on the form book.

As Mercer had pointed out several times, this desperate situation for England should never have arisen. But it had done so because in their match against Switzerland they had only managed to scramble a draw, while Holland and West Germany had been sharing the points and four goals in their game. Thus, with each having one match to play, West Germany had three points, England and Holland two each and Switzerland one point. By virtue of their present superior goal difference, West Germany were practically assured of reaching the final.

Mark hadn't expected to be picked for the Switzerland game, and he wasn't. The Boss had been furious about their misadventure on Thunersee and their 'irresponsibility' in accepting prolonged hospitality from Marc and his companions. It emerged that Terry Mercer *hadn't* given permission for them to have dinner at Marc's house and return as late as they did. When Marc had telephoned the college on the way back from Thunersee he had spoken not to Mr Mercer, as he had claimed, but to Doc Manton – and the physiotherapist insisted that Marc had merely said that the missing boys were safe and that they would be back at the training camp as soon as possible.

The blame for the affair had been apportioned most

unfairly, in Mark's opinion. For it was plain that the Boss held him to be the chief culprit. Mickey, he'd said, was not only the youngest, he was easily led by others who should have displayed more sense; and Keith was just as easily influenced 'by someone like you, Mark, who likes to do things in his own way.' Mark had felt like protesting strongly about that allegation but he'd guessed that it would avail him nothing. The trouble was that Keith could be something of a Jekyll and Hyde character: in the presence of authority he was usually subdued and malleable, but when he was with pals of his own age he could be assertive and self-willed. The upshot was that Mickey and Keith retained their places in the team against Switzerland, and, for the second successive time, Mark had been omitted: and on this occasion he hadn't even been named as substitute.

While Keith had been in his usual form, Mickey had had an indifferent match for once, and Mark couldn't help suspecting that it was due to the after-effects of his immersion in the lake. Fortunately, the Boss knew nothing about that: the one thing Mark and his room-mates could congratulate themselves on was that they'd managed to conceal news of that incident from the manager.

If Mark was to be selected for the match that afternoon, it would be at the expense, he worked out, of either Mickey or Billy Hilton. Kevin Bonnell's place was assured because he'd not only scored against Switzerland, he'd been easily the best of the forwards; and Tommy Archbold, in spite of his failure to score so far on the tour, was bound to be included if only for his ability to unsettle many defences and terrorise some.

Speed, according to Terry Mercer, was needed to slice open the German rearguard: speed in running, on and off the ball; speed in passing; speed in anticipation; speed in thought; speed in everything they attempted. That message had been hammered home so many times in the past few hours that Mark had just about given up listening. So, as it was being reiterated again, he nearly missed the follow-up: the announcement of the chosen team.

He was in! In his relief and excitement he felt like blasting one of the practice balls in to the furthest net. Then he caught Ian Wade's eye and realised that it was the midfield player who'd been dropped to make way for him. He gave Ian a sympathetic hunch of the shoulders. Then Terry Mercer came across and, taking him by the arm, steered him well away from the rest of the squad.

'I'm expecting a lot from you,' the Boss said, to Mark's amazement. He'd rather supposed that Mercer would say he was doing him a favour by playing him at all. 'I'm relying on your pace on the wing to open up their defence. That's why I want you to stay on the wide outside as much as possible. If they've got a weakness it's their right flank. They might be a bit cumbersome on the turn. You've got to exploit that– you and Mickey, that is.

'I want you to understand this, Mark. This is a team game and you're playing *with* the team, *for* the team. If you've got any ideas about taking on the entire German nation by yourself, forget them. O.K.?'

'Right, Boss,' Mark replied through his teeth. There was more he wanted to say, but discretion won.

'Good. I know you've got talent and I want to see it displayed out there this afternoon. Then perhaps we can forget all about the discreditable episodes of this tour.'

On that ominous note, he marched off towards Ian Wade, doubtless to explain exactly why he'd dropped him in favour of Mark Fox. Mickey, who'd feared that he'd be the one to be left out, was in excellent fettle again, and, as he kept saying, doubly happy to be resuming his partnership with Mark.

The rest of the squad were in a fairly subdued mood

111

at lunch, however, and the food itself didn't help. None of them was keen on poached fish. 'Bet the Germans are gnawing their way through best steak,' complained Keith. 'The Swiss dish up some pretty good steaks, you know. Well, *I* know they do.' Mark murmured warningly: 'Don't overdo it, Keith.' But the goalie just guffawed and said: 'Overdone steaks, you mean!' It seemed quite possible that Terry Mercer had overheard that. Still, Keith felt he was on safe ground: the one player whose confidence the Boss couldn't afford to damage was the goalkeeper.

Nerves seemed to be affecting all of them as they trotted out into bright sunlight and on to the emerald pitch. Because of a clash of colours, the teams had tossed for first choice; West Germany had won and therefore were in their normal white shirts and black shorts with England wearing red, a colour that had never been a favourite of Mark's. The stadium was the one in which they'd played their opening match but the crowd seemed smaller this time – though the vociferousness of the German supporters was certainly going to make up for that, judging by the manner in which they greeted their players. As Terry Mercer had pointed out, in German-speaking Zurich this would be like a home match for England's opponents.

After lining up for the national anthems to be played, followed by exchanges of emblems and a good deal of photography, the teams broke away for the customary shooting-in practice. Mark had taken in all that Terry Mercer had said about West Germany's goal-scoring star, Klaus Piepenburg, but his appearance was a surprise: below average height for his age, he had the stocky build of a rugby forward, with broad thighs and calf muscles that suggested great power. Digger Trowell, who'd been ordered not to give him a centimetre of freedom in the box, would tower above him. In contrast, the German captain and sweeper, Erich Schweninger, looked positively fragile:

112

willowy, drifting rather than running when he moved, and with an air of elegant disinterest in the proceedings.

Within a minute of the kick-off, all such conceptions had been exploded. From the whistle, Tommy surged ahead after slipping the ball to Kevin, who, instead of passing back, kept possession and then lobbed a pass back to Tommy. But Tommy, after rounding one opponent, couldn't control the ball. A German midfield player tapped it forward, veered to the right and then rolled the ball into space. With an electric burst, Schweninger snapped it up, dummied his way over the half-way line and then hit a perfectly judged pass to his left-winger.

David Redmile, who'd moved up in anticipation of an England attack, hesitated and then began to retreat. The winger went inside him and fled on a diagonal course. As Forster went in to challenge, the ball was fired hard to the corner of the box where Piepenburg had suddenly appeared. The German striker took the ball high on his chest, turned in almost a complete circle and then, as the ball dropped hit an unstoppable shot with his left foot high into the right-hand corner of the net. Afterwards, Keith admitted that he didn't even see the ball as it flew past him – and he was less than a metre off his line.

'Mein Gott!' Mark exclaimed aloud. It wouldn't have amused him to learn that several people in the crowd were saying precisely the same thing. The goal had been scored with such breath-taking speed and skill that it was some moments before the majority reacted at all – and then the entire stadium seemed to erupt.

Digger, who had been telling himself not to stray from his central line and had therefore seen little danger from where Piepenburg was positioned when the ball was crossed to him, simply looked stunned, as well he might. To be a goal down to a shot from that range, only thirty-eight seconds after the start, was practically beyond belief.

Schweninger had greeted the hero on the centre-line with open arms, but he himself deserved a share of the glory. After all, the way in which he'd started the movement that culminated in the goal had a brilliance of its own.

The shock-waves were evident as England kicked off again. Tommy Archbold stumbled over the ball as he played it to Kevin, who immediately lost it to a panther-like tackle from Piepenburg. The goal-scorer, in spite of appearing to be off-balance, hammered a pass out to the left-wing – and once again the flying winger faced a dithering England captain. His attempt at a tackle was crude and unfocused: he was rounded with contemptuous ease and, instantly the German assault forces were in full flow again. Digger, however, had recovered more quickly than his team-mates. When, following an exchange of passes, the ball was lobbed into the middle, it was the centre-back's head which butted it to a safe place. Nonetheless, Jimmy Kennan, trying to gain ground with a prodigious swing at the ball, simply belted it over the touch-line for a throw-in to his opponents.

By now, Terry Mercer was demonstrating that even he wasn't immune to some degree of neurosis. He had risen from his bench, advanced to the touch-line and was flapping his hands to indicate 'slow it down, play it cool'.

Easier semaphored than done. For the hard-running, incisive bursts from the West Germans was not at all what the England players had expected (or, as David Redmile muttered to Jimmy Kennan, 'been told to expect by the Great Mercer'). They'd thought their opponents would take time to warm up, swinging the ball about almost lazily, probing gently for an opening. The Germans had started as England meant to start. The confusion in the England ranks was considerable; and, because of his own evident inadequacy at present, their captain lacked the presence and authority that might have restored good order.

The next German raid was soon in progress. Schweninger, loping through the middle after picking up a ricochet from a tackle on Kevin, dummied beautifully past two opponents before swinging the ball out to the right. Deliberately – or so it seemed – he'd ignored Piepenburg's waving arm on the opposite flank. This time it was their other leading striker who was on the ball. He and Jimmy Kennan had a fine duel on the touch-line before the German shot free near the dead-ball line and pulled the ball back into the centre. The ubiquitous Schweninger was there to take it on his instep and then chip a pass with the utmost delicacy over Hilton's head. Digger, by now thoroughly perplexed by Piepenburg's roaming, charged in to tackle the man in possession – and that player simply stabbed the ball sideways. A team-mate pushed it forward obliquely as Redmile retreated – and suddenly Piepenburg had the ball again.

The shot, taken on the run and right-footed, was thunderous; the save was superb. Somehow, Keith had managed to finger-tip it over the bar, and was left wringing his hand for several minutes afterwards. The crowd roared their approval, for the shot as well as the save, but Piepenburg only looked annoyed that he hadn't burst the net. He continued to glower at Keith as the corner was taken; fortunately, the goalie didn't have to risk handling it this time, as Willett, one of the back four players, hooked the ball out of the area.

Mark, who still hadn't touched the ball, was in a familiar dilemma. When his side was under severe pressure he always felt he should drop back to help out in some way. But he guessed what the Boss's reaction would be if he did. He was being played as a striker, and a striker he must remain.

'If they keep this up, they'll beat us by a cricket score,' Mickey said as Mark jogged back to his wing territory. 'They're so *fast*, and so accurate.'

'We'll be just as good if only we get the ball,' Mark assured him. It was what he believed and wanted to prove.

But when at last the ball was directed out to England's left wing, Mickey, in his eagerness to control it and start up an attack, allowed it to bounce off his shin for a throw-in. Mark, covering the player most likely to receive the ball, nudged the boy off-balance. Unhesitatingly, the Italian referee awarded West Germany a free kick. Mark bit his lip and made no complaint. He was furious only with himself: committing a foul at his first attempt to win the ball was a stupid way to get into the game.

Tommy Archbold, at least as restless as all the other England forwards, eventually went in search of the ball, and, after managing to dispossess an opponent by sheer persistence, set off on one of his typical runs. Mark, not having expected the centre-forward to gain possession, was tardy in providing support. So it was Kevin who received a pass and took on the German defence by himself. But, in a clash with a full-back, the ball spun away from both of them. Mark, following up, reached it just as Schweninger arrived on the scene. Although he was still some distance outside the box Mark tried a snap shot. It was on target but not powerful enough to beat the yellow-shirted keeper who easily knocked it up, caught it and then cleared comfortably.

'Hard luck, Mark,' Mickey told him.

Mark shook his head. He knew he had reacted much too hastily. He should have taken the ball round the German captain and fired from much closer range. What he didn't like to admit to himself was that he'd been afraid that Schweninger would outwit him in some way. Already the

German display of skills was sapping the confidence of the opposition.

Only a minute later, England suffered another, and crucial, setback. Piepenburg, continuing in devastating form, was involved in a skirmish with Digger right on the edge of the box. He appeared to lose his balance, then recovered, only to go down again as the ball ran loose. In a trice he was on his feet again, yelling 'Elf-meter! Elf-meter!' Even those England players who'd never heard the phrase knew he was claiming a penalty kick. But, in the ensuing panic, Jimmy Kennan turned the ball over his own line for a corner instead. 'Ecke! Ecke!' he grinningly told the Germans, having at some time learned that this was the German for 'corner kick'. They still appealed vociferously for the penalty, but the referee overruled them and indicated that they should hurry up and take the corner.

The kicker judged it perfectly. The ball curled in tantalisingly and would have passed under the cross-bar but for Keith's leaping interception. As the keeper came down, Piepenburg, determined not to be thwarted this time, bustled in. Keith, twisting sinuously to get out of the way, hadn't seen that Digger, lungeing across in an effort to protect him from the German striker's attentions, was right in his path. And Keith, colliding heavily with the centre-back, went over backwards, still clutching the ball tightly to his chest. As he fell into the net the Germans' arms shot up like an instant forest.

The referee had no option but to award a goal, though he managed a sympathetic glance at the stricken goalkeeper as he did so. Digger was so horrified that he fell to his knees, his hands over his eyes. He wasn't alone in his grief. Despair was everywhere among the England players and officials.

Terry Mercer had turned away and was facing the crowd as if he couldn't bear to look at the scenes on the pitch;

but the sight of all those wildly waving red-black-yellow flags could only have been equally depressing.

'We've had it now,' remarked Mickey, and Mark didn't disagree. The West Germans would be the last players to relax just because they had a two-goal lead. So it proved: in the remaining minutes of the half they attacked as remorselessly as ever. The interval came as a relief only to the England defenders.

They'd expected the Boss to be angry. Instead, he came as near to being sympathetic as they'd ever known. There was no mention of any blame attaching to Digger and Keith for the second goal, and Mark was thankful at not being singled out among the forwards as having wasted the best scoring chance. Inevitably, the players themselves were subdued, and were drinking tea or fruit juice in comparative silence. Doc Manton went on his rounds offering glucose tablets and massage but got little response. When a club official popped his head round the dressing-room door, it was Mercer who went across to have a word with him. What he learned was the half-time score in the other match: Holland 2, Switzerland 0. It was the final blow, as he saw it. He didn't pass the news on to his players.

'Just go out there and do the very best you can,' he told them as they returned to the pitch. '*I* know you're capable of matching anything the opposition can achieve.'

Terry Mercer's words heartened them. They'd been expecting to be flayed: as it was, they felt uplifted. Almost at once, they broke through the German defensive wall. Tommy, hurling himself bodily at a cross from Mickey Hexton, forced the goalkeeper to make a scrambling save to prevent the ball from bouncing into the net near the far post. Digger raced up for the corner kick, got his head to the ball, nodding it down to Kevin, and then was unlucky not to score with a stabbing shot as the ball came back to him off a defender's ankle.

It was Digger, still venturing upfield at every opportunity in spite of the obvious need to shackle Klaus Piepenburg, who gave Mark his best opening yet. With a feint that left a defender prone on the surf, he cut inside, accelerating to go past another opponent who was beaten by sheer speed, and appeared to be heading straight for the box. Noting that Schweninger, who had been tending to cover his own right flank, was coming at him, Mark took the ball right up to him. Then he stopped dead. The German captain blinked in disbelief at such a deliberate confrontation. He was used to players releasing the ball the moment they realised he was going to challenge them.

To Mark's relief, no other opponent darted in to try and take the ball off him. His team-mates could scarcely believe that the great Schweninger was being teased in this way. After all, his reputation as one of the world's best teenage soccer players very nearly overawed *them*! Then, after what seemed like eternity to Mark but was really only seconds, Schweninger took a tentative step forward. As he did so, Mark rolled the ball back under his left foot, flicked it up and, with consummate skill, chipped a pass low over the German's head and into Mickey's path. Displaying great initial pace, Mickey raced on to the ball and hit it first time on the half-volley across the penalty area.

Tommy, reacting just as swiftly, tore in, and, striking when the ball was at ankle-height, smashed a shot towards goal. Once again, his luck was just out. For the ball grazed the outside of the post with the goalkeeper stranded, openmouthed, near his right-hand upright.

The crowd, irrespective of where their loyalties lay, applauded vigorously. It had been one of the very best moments of the game and there was no doubt that England were unfortunate not to have scored. Mark, thrilled that his trick had worked so well, commiserated with Tommy – and caught a narrow-eyed glance from Schweninger. He knew the German wouldn't let him get away with such an audacious manœuvre a second time.

Within a minute, Mark had the ball again, just inside the German half. A defender backed off as the England striker bore down on him, but Mark, changing his tactics, sent a curling pass to the wing with the outside of his right boot. Mickey took it easily in his stride before releasing it to Mark in a scissors movement. Once more, Schweninger was ideally placed to make an interception and this time he strode forward confidently. Mark, slowing to little more than a shuffle, leaned one way; and then, as the German checked, tilted the other way. Utterly confused and now off-balance as well, Schweninger was a victim ripe for nutmegging. Mark didn't hesitate. Flicking the ball neatly between the German's legs, he raced round his stricken adversary, collected the ball again and then whipped it into the middle. Tommy rose triumphantly, headed the ball sideways to Kevin – and, a split-second later, the goalie was beating down the shot at the second attempt. Then, as Kevin followed up, the ball was somehow diverted to another defender who unceremoniously thumped it over the line for a relief-giving corner.

In spite of another determined effort by Digger, England were unable to force the ball into the net. Nonetheless, their attacks became constant and it seemed to be only a matter of time before they got a goal. Kevin, displaying more industry in half an hour than he usually showed in three matches, was twice thwarted by desperate last-ditch tackles when it appeared certain that he was about to score. Mickey regularly took defenders on and frequently outpaced and outwitted them, but still no one was able to turn his centres into the net. Tommy, often combining with Kevin in beautifully timed one–twos, was hitting shots from all angles, only to find that the German goalkeeper possessed brilliance as well as luck. Mark was revelling in his duel with Schweninger: he couldn't fail to because he was winning it. The German skipper, however, refused to accept that: wherever Mark went, he fellowed – and his was always the first challenge when Mark had possession.

The fear was that with so many England players committed to attack, their opponents would get a breakaway goal and put the issue beyond recall. Piepenburg, no longer under close surveillance by Digger, was roving all over the place. At last, from a prodigious clearance, the ball reached him. Piepenburg, on the right flank, instantly had it under control and raced into the box.

Keith reacted with the same speed. With no team-mate able to cut off the German's approach, he had to come out. As the striker veered to his left to go round him, Keith swooped, snatching the ball practically off a toecap and then, astonishingly, somersaulted back on to his feet. Without pause, he threw the ball in a fast overhand movement to Jimmy Kennan who, belatedly, was running back to help. Jimmy, too, reacted swiftly, swinging his foot under the ball to hook it back upfield towards Mark Fox.

Schweninger, his role as sweeper long abandoned, was within a metre of him as Mark, hovering on the halfway line, took a step towards the ball. Automatically, Schweninger moved after him. Suddenly, Mark ducked, allowing the ball to bounce over his shoulder; and, as it did so, he spun round and hared after it. The trick was Mark's favourite, one that he'd perfected over the past few seasons, and it took the German captain completely by surprise. He set off in pursuit, but by now Mark had gone clear, the ball at his feet.

This time Mark had only one aim: to go straight for goal. In anticipation of a goal from Piepenburg, the German midfielders had moved forward; the electric speed with which the ball had been transferred from England goalkeeper to England striker caught them out of position.

Mark, not deviating from his chosen path except to swerve round a full-back, burst into the box. He picked his spot as the goalkeeper advanced and hit the ball with all the power he possessed in his left foot. In the same moment, the goalkeeper courageously leapt forward and upwards in the hope of making contact with the ball somehow.

The ball struck him on his shoulder and its force was enough to knock him over. Mark had not stopped moving forward. As the ball, which had shot high into the air, fell towards him, Mark nimbly hurdled the prostrate goalkeeper and nodded it confidently into the unguarded net.

He had done it! He had scored for England.

Overjoyed, he leapt high in the air and then, clasping his hands above his head, turned to receive the congratulations of his team-mates. Inevitably, it was Mickey who was first on the scene to hug him with delight.

'Fantastic goal, Mark! Must be the best anyone's scored in the whole tournament.'

Mark had never felt happier in his life. He had achieved his ambition in the most glorious fashion. All the disappointments of the past few weeks could be forgotten. For, as he saw when he glanced towards the touch-line, even Terry Mercer was still on his feet and applauding the goal-scorer.

There was scarcely time for the Germans to kick off again before the referee, with several trills and flamboyant gestures, signalled the end of the match. The second half had been played at such a furious pace, with few stoppages for anything, that it was some moments before even the Germans realised that it was over. Then they set off on a lap of honour, responding exuberantly to the flag-waving and prolonged cheering of their supporters.

As his team left the pitch, Terry Mercer was waiting to shake each player by the hand. The fact that England were now out of the tournament must have been uppermost in

122

his mind but he wasn't allowing that to cancel out his pleasure in the way his boys had played in the second half. They had put on an exhilarating performance.

'That was a brilliant goal, Mark,' he said with obvious sincerity. 'You made it and you took it magnificently. We may have lost the match but you've given us all something to remember – for a long, long time.'

Chapter Ten

THE MYSTERY MAN

As they waited at the airport for their flight to be called, many of the England Juniors' squad drifted around in search of final souvenirs. The depression that had settled on them after the defeat by West Germany had lifted: most of the players, though they wouldn't care to admit it, were glad to be going home. They'd played in an international tournament, had some memorable experiences in a supremely beautiful country and had a lot of stories to tell. Soon, too, the summer holidays would be starting. In spite of his team's playing record, even Terry Mercer looked quite cheerful. He'd told the boys that he was heartened by the way they'd fought back against the Germans, and added that he hoped one day they'd all be together again as a senior England squad.

Mark, wandering past some glittering displays of watches and jewellery in company with Mickey, had mixed feelings. It had been a disappointment to play in only one full game for England, and, worse still, to score a goal for Holland. On the other hand, it couldn't be denied he'd wiped out that terrible blunder by scoring England's only goal in the last match. Because of his friendship with Keith and Mickey, he'd also run foul of the manager. But, they'd since been assured, their escapade at Thunersee was now a closed book. The manager was willing to forget it as long as they never did anything so foolish again. His generosity had surprised and gratified them. 'Perhaps,' Keith had remarked thoughtfully, 'he's not such a bad bloke after all.' Then the goalie had added with a characteristic grin: 'But then, we didn't let him down in the last match, did we? I mean, we all played pretty well, didn't we.' Neither of his confederates was going to dispute that.

Mark's performance against West Germany had been one of the real highlights of the tour (Terry Mercer himself had said so, publicly). His triumph over Schweninger, regarded everywhere as the most outstanding young player in Europe and a future captain of West Germany, had been total. After the match, Schweninger had shaken his hand and said, with a forced grin: 'Next time we meet, I will know better how to play against you, Mark.'

Suddenly, Mark was shaken out of his reverie. Mickey had grabbed his arm and was muttering: 'Oh no, no, no! He's here again and he's seen us.'

As Mark looked round, he spotted a man approaching him: the man they'd seen the day they arrived in Zurich, the man who'd caused Mickey to panic at Thun, the man who, again, was wearing a pale blue jacket and a peaked cap. Mickey, he sensed, was on the point of fleeing. Now it was Mark who held him back. 'No, Mickey, let's see what he wants. He can't cause any trouble here. There're too many people about.'

'Pardon, please,' the man was saying with a rather shy attempt at a smile. 'You are English? I know, yes. So, please, can you help me? I am a student of English. I wish – '

'Look, what do you want?' Mark retaliated aggressively. 'Why have you been following us about all over the place? What do you think you're doing?'

The man looked stunned. 'Following you? I do not understand.'

Crisply Mark pointed out that he had even followed them to Thun.

'Oh, no, please,' the fellow protested, plainly embarrassed by such an accusation. 'That was a – a accident – how do you say? – oh, a *coincidence*. I was really surprised to see you there, very surprised. It was my day off work and I go often to Thun. I did not expect to see you there.'

Mark was still not convinced, though the man now did seem harmless enough. 'Well, what do you want?' he demanded.

'A little help, that is all. I wish to understand the meaning of the word "welter". A difficult word, I think. Can you explain, please, what it means?'

Mark was so taken aback by the unexpectedness, and the simplicity, of the request that for a moment he could not think how to answer. But his suspicions were evaporating rapidly. The inquiry appeared to be a genuine one.

'Well,' he answered at last, 'it means something heavy, really. There's a welter-weight in boxing. He would be one of the heavier and bigger fighters.'

'Ah, so! Now I understand,' said the man, now with a serious expression on his face. He had taken a small black notebook from his pocket and was writing in it. 'Thank you. You are very kind.'

'But why do you want to know that?' asked Mickey, summoning up enough courage to speak for the first time.

'I wish to speak English very correctly. I wish to work here at the airport. I would like that very much. When my English is excellent I may get that job. Yes?'

125

Their flight number was being announced over the loud-speakers. 'Hey, we'll have to go,' Mark said. 'But good luck with the job!'

They all shook hands and then the boys headed for the departure lounge to join up with their team-mates.

'You see, Mickey, I told you that bloke was harmless enough,' Mark pointed out. 'You'll have to snap out of that idea that the whole world's against you. Most people are quite O.K. if you treat 'em right.'

It was when they were all lining up for a security check before going out to the plane that Mark remembered something. 'Still got your money belt on, Mickey?'

'Sure,' Mickey replied, patting his thigh. 'Only it's empty now. Not a single franc left. So it wouldn't matter if I did lose it.'

Mark was surprised. Mickey had spent very little when they'd been together, though one day he'd gone off on his own on a special shopping expedition. 'What did you buy, Mickey?'

'Presents for all the boys at the Home, one for each of them. You see, I've been lucky to have this trip to Switzerland. None of them has ever been abroad. So I thought I should take them some souvenirs. In a funny way, they're my family – the only one I've got, anyway. And you bought presents for your family, didn't you?'

Mark had completely forgotten that Mickey would be returning to the orphanage. He stopped in his tracks and faced the younger boy.

'Mickey, I've had a thought. Why don't you come and stay with us for a few days during the holiday? I know my parents would be happy to have you – truly.'

Mickey's eyes glowed. 'Do you mean it, Mark? That would be great!'

'Of course I mean it. And we could do some training together, practise a few new moves.'

Mickey was nodding excitedly. 'We could also go along to one of the big clubs and ask if they'd give us a trial. You never know, they might even want to sign us on.'

'That,' said Mark thoughtfully, 'is a good idea. A *very* good idea. In fact, it's brilliant, I mean, how could it fail when we tell 'em we've both played for England?'

'And both scored goals for England,' added Mickey eagerly. 'Don't forget that.'

Mark nodded. 'Oh, I won't forget that. As long as I live, I'll never forget the first goal I scored for England.'

has a whole shipload of exciting books for you

Armadas are chosen by children all over the world. They're designed to fit your pocket, and your pocket money too. They're colourful, gay, and there are hundreds of titles to choose from. Armada has something for everyone:

Mystery and adventure series to collect, with favourite characters and authors – like Alfred Hitchcock and The Three Investigators. The Hardy Boys. Young detective Nancy Drew. The intrepid Lone Piners. Biggles. The rascally William – and others.

Hair-raising spinechillers – ghost, monster and science fiction stories. Super craft books. Fascinating quiz and puzzle books. Lots of hilarious fun books. Many famous children's stories. Thrilling pony adventures. Popular school stories – and many more exciting titles which will all look wonderful on your bookshelf.

You can build up your own Armada collection – and new Armadas are published every month, so look out for the latest additions to the Captain's cargo.

If you'd like a complete, up-to-date list of Armada books, send a stamped, self-addressed envelope to:

Armada Books,
14 St James's Place,
London SW1A 1PF